The Moralist II

More tales of people and events in Centerfield, Texas, during a year recently concluded.

John Warley

The Moralist II

More tales of people and events in Centerfield, Texas, during a year recently concluded.

By John Warley

John Warley

Other works by John Warley

Fiction
Bethesda's Child
The Moralist
A Southern Girl (Story River Books, Pat Conroy, editor, a University of South Carolina Press Imprint 2014)

Non-Fiction
Stand Forever, Yielding Never;
The Citadel in the 21st Century (Evening Post Books 2018)

Published Essays
"Lingering at the Doors" (*This I Believe on Fatherhood*, Jossey-Bass, A Wiley Imprint 2011)
"One Cadet's Lamentations" (*Our Prince of Scribes*, University of Georgia Press, forthcoming 2018)

Dedication

To Michael S. Mulkey, Esq., my former law partner
and as fine a man as I have known.

John Warley

Our story so far . . .

Fran, a widow with three kids (Chip, James and Sarah) and an uncommon amount of common sense. She edits the Centerfield newspaper, *The Sentinel*, owned by Ed Abernathy.

George and Joyce Fafalone, Fran's wealthy but clueless next-door neighbors who own the house Fran rents.

Kirstin Fafalone, George and Joyce's daughter who Fran sets straight. She was dating a biker, Pete, when she met Jeff and wised up.

Scott Fafalone, George and Joyce's high school son who has a fetish for women's orthopedic shoes.

Abraham Rubiwitz (a/k/a Art Adams), an Israeli citizen sent to Texas to buy the land that will eventually encompass New Israel.

Tricksy Faye Dogget, a sexy deputy clerk in the Centerfield courthouse that Abe/Art develops a serious crush on.

Ed Abernathy, owner of *The Sentinel* newspaper, Fran's boss, and a serial womanizer who spends his time playing golf and chasing skirts.

Todd Melville, a wealthy conservative who wooed Fran but is married.

Mamoud Abbar (a/k/a Monty Archer), a Palestinian resident of Texas who owns the Porkrind Trust.

The Porkrind Trust, a legal entity created to establish New Palestine in Texas. It owns 10,000 acres in the middle of the land Abe/Art has accumulated for New Israel.

Buster Bustamonte, a retired professional baseball player who defeated Fran for Mayor of Centerfield.

"Ed's Barbeque Butter," the brand name Ed intends to use to market a concoction he discovered in a barbeque contest he judged.

Chapter 1

George is Reminded that Life Can be the Pits

Fran emerged from her house in a robe and slippers to get *The Sentinel*. As she checked the headline she herself had written twelve hours earlier, her eyes diverted to Hobbit Lane, where the road intersected her driveway. Where pavement should have been, a giant hole gaped up at her. It was as if the surface had been hit by a meteor. She walked to the edge and peered down. It was at least fifteen feet deep and had consumed both lanes and the white line. She called Centerfield's public works number.

Her call was answered by Ernesto Bustamonte. Since Buster's election as mayor, a remarkable number of city employees seemed to be named Bustamonte. She told him it looked to her like a sinkhole.

"In Texas?" he said. "Are you sure you are not in Florida?"

"Quite sure," Fran said. "I'm right here in Centerfield."

"I guess we should do something."

"That would be a start."

"I will send over our best supervisor."

"Who is?"

"Hector Bustamonte. Very good man. He can

be there after lunch."

"I highly recommend someone come sooner, if for no other reason than to put up some barricades. A car driving in there will never come out."

Fran recruited Chip, who was getting ready for school. Together they placed trash cans, a step ladder, a lawn mower and a bicycle around the pit to warn approaching motorists. The road was lightly traveled, serving a few houses including Fran's rental and George and Joyce next door. She had just sent Chip back to the garage for more temporary impediments when she heard George's mechanized gate open and his Lexus came roaring out of his driveway headed straight for disaster. Because he was eating a chocolate covered éclair and talking on his cell phone, he didn't see the bicycle or lawnmower until he hit them, knocking both into the pit. He slammed on his brakes and skidded toward the edge. His front tires lipped the edge and came to rest over the hole. Only the scraping of his undercarriage kept the car from plunging. The car teetered precariously, a breath away from a nose dive. George powered down his window and looked south. "Damn!" he exclaimed. "I'm going to die."

"Only if you shift your weight forward," Fran yelled.

He had not notice her until now.

"What should I do?" he asked.

"Stay very still. I'll go inside to call a wrecker to pull you out."

"Yeah, well tell them to hurry. Old man Posey died last night, and the family is coming in to make arrangements. This will be a fifty-thousand-dollar death minimum. Golden stiffs, we call them, but don't repeat that." He looked down again. "Someone is gonna get sued over this."

"Perhaps Mother Nature," Fran said. "It must have happened just before I got up, but I never heard a thing. Just walked out to get the paper and found it."

"Looks like a bomb crater," he said, wiping chocolate from his mouth.

Fran went into her house and emerged two minutes later. "Big Al is on the way."

But when Big Al arrived twenty minutes later, he noticed something neither Fran nor George had considered. Because mature mesquite trees lined the road leading to the houses, the wrecker could not get around the pit to position itself behind George's car. The pit spanned the road from a wall surrounding George's house to the tree line. George was trapped.

"So what do I do?" George asked, sweat beading on his forehead. "Sit here all day while the Poseys decide that cremation is a better option? I'm losing money here."

Big Al stood six-three, weighed about 150, and when he stood looked more or less like the letter "S". He called to George over the pit. "Crawl into the back seat and get out the back door." He winked at Fran.

"Very funny, Al," George said.

"Only a couple of other options," Al said, rubbing his weathered chin. "We could call in Hercules Helicopter. They do big lifts—heavy duty air conditioners and stuff like that. They could rig a sling that would hold the car and lift it out. Problem is they're out of Houston and I'm sure we could get them by the end of the week."

"You're killing me, Al. What's the other option?"

"Blow torch the top. Make it a convertible, so to speak. Then you could ease your way into the back seat and over the trunk."

"You want to blowtorch the roof of an eighty thousand-dollar Lexus?"

"You got any better ideas?"

"I do," Fran said. "An industrial crane can reach across and lift the car and George out."

"There," said George with obvious relief. "I'm glad someone around here is thinking. Benny's Industrial leases those things. I'll call Benny now. We buried his brother last year. A beautiful service with some rented angels singing nice stuff. He owes me."

George picked up his cell phone and punched the screen with a stubby finger. "Benny? George Fafalone. I'm in a bind over here at the house. I need one of your cranes. A big one . . . yeah, kinda hard to explain . . . no, you probably need to come see the situation for yourself . . . hurry, will you? I got a big meeting today . . . you know where I live . . . yeah, okay, thanks." George felt his blood pressure begin to climb; hell, it had been climbing since his first peak down, but only now did it register with the force of Texas heat in mid-drought. A spot behind his frontal lobe began to demand his attention, in the way someone repeatedly hitting your big toe with a ball peen hammer demands your attention. Of even greater concern was the pulsing beneath his left bicep. In the weeks leading up to his heart attack, that same vein had throbbed relentlessly. And if he had a cardiac episode here, how would the EMS people get to him, or he to them? Don't panic, he told himself. Think about something pleasant, like the Posey funeral.

While they waited for Benny, Fran and Al snaked a rope over the rear axle, careful not to disturb the car's delicate equilibrium. They secured the ends of the rope to a tree. At least now they had some small insurance against the car pitching over, assuming the rope held.

Ten minutes later Benny stood at the edge of the pit looking across. He gave out a low whistle. "Nice piece of driving, George. I guess you couldn't see the hole since it's only thirty feet wide."

George huffed. "Can you get me out or not?"

Benny grinned. "Sure I can. It won't be cheap, but neither was my brother's funeral."

An hour later, as Fran and Al looked on, Benny returned with two of his workmen and a huge crane on the back of a flatbed truck. Unloading the crane and stabilizing it took another hour, as did positioning the boom, rigging the sling, and cradling it beneath George's car. When all was in place, the crane roared to life, lifting the car and George skyward. When they were suspended ten feet off the ground, Benny killed the crane's motor in order to be heard.

"I forgot to ask, George. Which side of the hole do you want to come down on?"

"I need the car," George fumed. "Put me down on the other side."

"You got it," said Benny, clearly enjoying this assignment. Minutes later the car rested on the road again. George got out to inspect the damage. "Could have been worse," he said to Fran.

She agreed. "How long will it take them to repair this? My car will be useless until the hole is filled and the road repaved. It could be weeks."

"You know, Fran, I came to a decision sitting there today, hanging in the air and good puff of wind away from disaster."

"And what was that?" she asked.

"I was wedged into my seat and couldn't move because I'm too damn fat."

Fran raised her eyebrows in mock surprise.

"Yep, I'm going to do it," he said.

"A real diet?" she asked.

"I tried that. Those things don't work. I'm going for liposuction. I'll beat this weight thing yet."

Seeing how seriously George related this epiphany, Fran suppressed a grin. "Sounds like a plan," she said. "And now I need to get to work."

"I'll give you a lift," George offered.

"Thanks, but I'll ride my bike. That way I'll have a ride back. And from the looks of this pit, I better get used to it because I have a feeling this problem isn't going away anytime soon."

Chapter 2

Ed brushes up on his Latin

The bike ride from Fran's house to the offices of *The Sentinel* took twenty minutes. She waved at Kirstin as she entered. Kirstin looked up from her keyboard, waved back, and continued typing. In the hallway Fran ran into Ed, the owner.

"You won't believe the morning I've had," Fran said.

"Well, why don't you come on back to my office, sit in my lap, and tell me about it."

"Ed, don't you ever give up?"

"No, should I?"

"Yes. And there are those little things called sexual harassment laws."

"Not in Texas. In this state, it's cavalier emperor or whatever that Latin is that means 'what Ed wants Ed is going to get unless you don't want Ed to have it more than Ed wants to get it.' It's amazing how them Latins got so much into two words."

"The phrase is caveat emptor, and it has nothing to do with sex."

"Then I've been misinformed. What happened this morning?"

Fran related finding the sinkhole, George's narrow escape, and the fact that she was now without automotive transportation until the repairs were completed. "But don't worry," she told him, I'll find a way to get here. What's a few days of inconvenience? Besides, the bike is great exercise."

"I gotta see the hole," Ed said. "Come on. We can ride over in my car."

"Maybe the guy from the city will be there. They are supposed to be placing barricades around it so someone even less attentive than George doesn't take a header into it."

They drove to Fran's. As Ed stood at the edge, marveling at the length and breadth of the pit, a city car pulled up. From it emerged a man shorter than Fran and very stocky, with a neatly trimmed mustache. He put on a cowboy hat as he greeted them.

The newcomer extended his hand. "Hector Bustamonte, at your service."

After introductions, they all walked to the precipice. Bustamonte shook his head. "I have never seen such a thing before. Not in Texas. Not even in Mexico, where I thought I saw everything. I wonder what could cause such a thing as this."

"Beats me," Fran said. "As you can see my son and I tried to put up some warning obstacles, but my neighbor nearly drove into it this morning.

"And you heard nothing in the night?"

"Nothing. Quiet, as usual."

"Very strange," said Hector, removing his cowboy hat to scratch his head. "First, we will put up some proper barricades with flashing lights and reflectors. Then, I will alert the superintendent of the public works department."

"Who is that?" Ed asked.

"That is Jorge Bustamonte. A very good man."

"Are you related?" Fran wanted to know.

"He is my cousin."

"And are you also related to the mayor?"

"He is also my cousin."

"I see," said Fran. "Well, I hope Mr. Jorge Bustamonte can get the repairs done quickly. This road is the only access my neighbors and I have to town."

"I understand. When he played soccer, they called him Speedy, so I am sure he will move right away."

"Good," said Fran. "I feel better." She turned to Ed. "I guess this qualifies as news. I'll send a photographer over to get some shots." Ed nodded as if the thought had not occurred to him, as indeed it had not.

By nightfall, wooden barricades had been placed around the pit and, as promised by Hector Bustamonte, flashing lights and reflectors as well. The lights cast an eerie red glow on the interior walls of Fran's house. She pulled the shades in her bedroom, which muted the glow but there it was, bleating on and off, on and off, like a neon hotel sign from an old B movie starring what's his name.

The following morning, a pickup truck with the

town seal emblazoned on the door drove up. From it stepped Jorge Bustamonte, a rotund man with a baby face and a receding hairline who resembled Hector not in the least. Fran noticed at once his delicate hands and fingers; the kind she would associate with a concert pianist and not a fleet soccer player. His grin revealed perfect teeth as he introduced himself.

"And now," he said, "let me examine this most unusual site I have heard much about from my cousin, Hector."

Fran watched as Jorge pulled a ladder from the pickup, placed it into the pit, and climbed down. He walked around the floor, picked up some loose clods and rubbed them between his hands. He brought the residue to his nose, sniffing. Then he turned his attention to the nearest wall. He took a pen from his pocket, poking and prodding while dirt fell at his feet. He seemed to be keeping one eye on the space above him, where a chunk of the highway looked as if it was capable of falling without much urging. From a side pocket he extracted a small magnifying glass and studied the cavity he had created in the wall, bringing it to within inches of the surface. He nodded several times, then climbed the ladder.

"Most unusual," he told Fran. "The caliche appears much more porous than we see in this part of Texas."

"And the caliche is . . .?"

"In a word, calcium carbonate. I guess that's

two words. Centerfield is largely situated on a strata of caliche, part of the Goliad Formation from the Miocene period. This hole could indicate an instability in the soil that we didn't suspect."

Fran said, "Pardon my curiosity, but do all supervisors of public works learn such things as part of their training?"

Jorge Bustamonte laughed. "Oh, no. That comes from my study of geology. I taught it at SMU before coming here."

"That seems an odd background for public works. Where did you study engineering?"

Jorge laughed again, his perfect white teeth flashing. "I didn't. Math and the like bore me."

"But doesn't your job demand that?"

"I have people for that. No, Cousin Buster wished me to join his team, so I resigned from SMU to come here. Better hours, better pay, less stress. Faculty politics is the worst. As we like to say, the fights are so bitter because the stakes are so small."

Now Fran laughed. "I'll remember that one. So, when do you think your people can begin the repairs?"

Jorge gazed back at the pit. "I will need to take some soil samples. Once the results come back, we will know more. We must be certain of the cause of this most unusual phenomena. When that is determined, we may be able to predict when and where other sinkholes will appear."

Fran sighed audibly. "That doesn't sound quick

and easy."

"We will put our best people on it. You will have a new road before you know it." He turned, retrieved the ladder from the pit, and waved farewell.

Fran turned again to Ed. "Why do I feel so strongly that this hole is going to become a feature of the neighborhood?"

"Because the city is in charge of fixing it?"

Chapter 3

Tricksy Visits the North Pole

When it was learned that the Palestinians owned 10,000 acres in the middle of what was to be New Israel, Art's hopes of receiving his fat commissions took a left turn. In fact, he was now short on money, as his per diem was hardly the kind of cash needed to keep Tricksy happy. But being the independent woman Tricksy was, she proposed to take a second job rather than slash expenses.

"What will you do?" Art asked.

"Get a night job."

"Doing exactly what?"

"Art, darlin', there are just so many positions open for a gal with my qualifications. I need something that has a lot of payback for not a whole lot of work. Are you with me?

"No."

"How would you feel about your little love button becoming an exotic dancer?" She cupped her breasts. "It will keep these puppies in good condition and I know you'll like that. If I can get the early shift I can be home by 10 with a wad of cash. Mostly ones and fives."

"This exotic dancing—is it . . . dignified?"

"Relax. You'll love it. I set up an audition down at the North Pole."

The North Pole was an oddity even by Centerfield standards. It had begun its corporate life as a Christmas shop, where lights, bulbs, trees, tinsel, wrap, cards, rooftop figures, crèches and all things Santa Claus were sold. The store made enough money in December to more than justify the bleak months leading up to Christmas. It was owned by Reverend Jeremiah Clingenpeel, a Baptist minister, who possessed strong entrepreneurial tendencies (along with some other tendencies) and who somewhat shamelessly proselytized his business from the pulpit. Beginning on the Sunday after Thanksgiving, he exhorted his parishioners to deck their halls and their walls and their tables and their bedrooms and their yards and their cars with what he called "the gladness of the season." Everyone at Free Will Baptist got a fifteen percent discount during December, a generous layaway plan, and an interest loaded charge account.

The good reverend was a handsome man, with brownish skin that looked like deep tan but was in fact genetic. His skin was nicely accented by silver hair, so in the pulpit he appeared a bit like God were He a Baptist with a LA haircut. Unknown to his congregation (and to the reverend himself until some intensive psychoanalysis in his mid-twenties), he had been abused as a child by a babysitter who punished bad behavior by compelling him to eat Hostess Twinkies to the point of nausea. The sitter did other things as well, but no one wants to read the details of child abuse, so let's just say the reverend had some "issues" that gave him a dark side he kept well disguised.

But as time went on, as time will do, the internet and big box stores like Wall-More took their toll, profits declined, and Reverend Clingenpeel became increasingly fixated on finding an alternative revenue source. Which helps explains why the good reverend applied for a liquor license, which was issued to the North Pole on the condition that the license was valid only after six p.m. And even though gambling was something preached against on a regular basis, Reverend Clingenpeel took a big gamble in the form of capital improvements. He went to great expense to reinforce his countertops and have runway lights installed. He spent a small fortune on the sound system, with the utmost in woofers, tweeters and amplifiers.

And then there was the matter of the pole itself. Unwilling to order just any pole from a random supplier, the reverend embarked on a six months tour of Texas, inspecting every pole he could locate and, in an impressive display of due diligence, interviewing the women who used the poles. He asked extensive questions about grip and width. Should the surface be smooth and highly polished, or slightly buffed for better traction? He noticed that the women seemed more forthcoming when he bought them drinks during the interviews, and soon questions about the poles led logically to questions about performance attire and the suppliers thereof. Yes, with the large amount of money he was investing in the North Pole, he was leaving no stone unturned, no question unasked, and no cleavage uninspected.

In the first year of the North Pole's duel (some said schizophrenic) existence, the store closed at five p.m. from January through November, and at six in December. The evening shift cleared the counters of Christmas stuff, opened the bar, and snuffed out the nerve-grating Jingle Bells and Deck the Halls that alternated incessantly during regular hours. Performers entered through a rear door that led into what had been a storage area but was converted, again at great expense, into dressing cubicles, complete with hidden cameras that allowed Reverend Clingenpeel to monitor smoking, which he strictly forbade.

Monday was the one day of the week that the North Pole closed to evening business. The weekends proved so busy, and Mondays so flat, that it made economic sense to give the staff that day off. It was also the day Reverend Clingenpeel auditioned new talent and the day Tricksy showed up to apply for the job. She wore a very demure see-through blouse that caused the Reverend's eyes to widen as she introduced herself. He handed her the official North Pole g-string, part of a holly leaf on the front and a tiny bell on either side that tinkled as its wearer performed. The pasties were snowflakes. Tricksy retreated to the dressing room and changed into her new uniform while Clingenpeel observed through the hidden camera to make certain she was not a secret smoker. She did some basic stretching, then re-appeared for her first encounter with the pole (smooth and highly polished). Clingenpeel decided to hire her during the introductory bars to the first song, but out of courtesy let her complete her routine.

"That was quite an impressive performance," he said to her.

"I believe in giving it my all," she said.

"Your all is a lot," he said. "Have you thought about your performance name? Our employees find it advisable to use stage names when they work."

Tricksy nodded. "Oh, you mean names like Misty and Crystal and Dawn."

"Exactly."

"I have given it some thought," she said, tapping a manicured nail on the counter where the runway lights still flashed. "You want your stage name to be different. It's kind of like you step out of your own skin when you're up on the pole. Like you're someone else."

"Most of our ladies say the same thing," Clingenpeel agreed.

"And that's why I picked Sue Collins."

Clingenpeel's jaw went slack. "Sue Collins?"

"What's the matter, is it taken?"

"Ah . . . no, no one else uses it. Are you sure you

don't want something more . . . exotic?"

"When you're born with a name like mine, Sue sounds pert damn exotic to me."

"Okay, then," he said. "Sue Collins it is. Can you start Friday night?"

Chapter 4

Fran Negotiates World Peace

The day after Tricksy was hired to work nights at the North Pole, Fran rose early to begin what was certain to be a long day. Art Adams (nee Abe Rubiwitz) and Monty Archer (nee Mamoud Abbar) had each agreed to meet Fran at the offices of *The Sentinel*, but they had not agreed to meet with each other. Fran hoped to bring about such a meeting, and to mediate it once the two men were together.

As she retrieved the paper from her driveway, she looked into the pit to see what progress had been made on repairs. A quick inspection confirmed there had been exactly none. She jotted herself a mental note to call the city again to press the matter. She saw George's Lexus parked at one of the barricades. Getting to and from his house required George to walk along the edge of the pit, through the mesquite trees, and he muttered oaths on every trip because he did not enjoy the effort required to walk fifty yards. Nor did he like having to carpool with Joyce, whose car was, like Fran's, essentially useless until the road was repaired.

Fran biked to *The Sentinel*. Along the way she saw evidence of Centerfield's gradual growth—growth that would make her paper a daily in the near future. There was a new dry cleaner, an IHOP, a Burger King across from a new McDonald's, a Denny's, three Starbucks, and a weight loss clinic. She arrived at her office a half hour before Art and Monty, giving strict instructions that they were to be shown to separate conference rooms.

Art arrived first, decked out in his ten-gallon hat, boots, and a new string tie held in place by a steer's head. He looked worried and apprehensive. Kirstin greeted him, escorted him to Conference Room A, and brought coffee. Monty arrived ten minutes later, dressed in a white cotton shirt and jeans. He was taken to Conference Room B.

Since Fran had never met Monty, she greeted him first and served coffee. He seemed pleasant enough, telling her he had voted for her in the mayoral election and that he read the paper front-to-back every week.

"Everyone in town says you are a fair person," Monty said. "That is why I am hoping you can help me resolve this problem with the Jew."

"You're schmoozing me, but it is working," she said. "I hope I can be helpful, but I see no way of resolving the issues without the active participation of Art Adams, which is why I've asked him to come today also."

"The Jew is here, in this building?"

"Just down the hall."

"Aha!" he said. "This explains why I have been put in Conference Room B. The Jew must be in

Conference Room A, no doubt a better one with a view and bottled water."

Fran opened the sluice gate to the reservoir of patience she knew she would need to deal with Monty and Art. "Mr. Adams was shown to Conference Room A because he arrived first. The conference rooms are exactly alike. There is no view because there are no windows. Bottled water is available upon request. Would you like some?"

Monty grumbled that he would think about it, then said something under his breath that sounded to Fran like "a slight to my people." She let it pass.

She sat opposite him at the conference table. "The purpose of today's meeting," she said, "is to introduce you to Art, to review the best interests of both parties in resolving this quickly and fairly, and to determine a future course of dealing."

"So it is not enough that we are in the same building. You want me to meet with a Jew?" Monty asked.

"Yes. And I want him to meet with you. The three of us will meet together."

"But what about the right of return and secure borders?"

"Don't you think it is a bit premature to discuss those issues? We've just had coffee."

"Look," said Monty, "you seem like a very nice lady, and I appreciate what you are trying to do. So I will cooperate fully with one condition, and that is that I will not agree to anything that Jew wants.

Other than that, everything is negotiable."

"I see," said Fran. "The important thing today is to meet, to review a few things, and to plot a future course. So can I assume you are willing to meet with Art Adams? He is a nice man."

"Where will this meeting take place?"

"In Conference Room A."

"No. He must come here. To Conference Room B. I must be very firm on this."

Fran nodded. "I will speak with him now."

In Conference Room A, she asked Art to join her and Monty in Conference Room B.

"Did you inspect him?" Art wanted to know. "Did he remove his shirt? They wear exploding vests, those Arabs do. I think he should go through security—twice."

"We don't have 'security,' Fran said. "And I feel confident he is not wearing anything that will explode. You have my assurance on that. So, will you join us in Conference Room B?"

"No. It is an insult to Judaism to have to grovel to him. He can come here."

"Is it that important?" she asked.

"If I give in on this point, he will want the West Bank."

"The West Bank of what?"

"Of San Pedro Creek."

"The last time I drove over the creek it was dry."

"Yes, and if it is again wet they will drain the

water. You cannot trust an Arab."

Fran eyed him steadily. "We have two conference rooms here; A and B. Only two. One of you will have to come to the other. Suppose we flip a coin to decide."

"You will flip the coin?"

"Yes, I will flip the coin."

"In the spirit of cooperation and for the future of my people, I will agree to that."

"Good. Let me speak with Monty. Mr. Archer."

On confirming that Fran would flip the coin, Monty agreed, and so the two men were brought together in Fran's office and introduced. It did not, in Fran's view, get off to an auspicious start when they refused to shake hands, Monty called Art a "blood-sucker," and Art returned the pleasantry by calling Monty a "stone age thief."

"Gentlemen," Fran said smoothly. "I write the editorials in Centerfield, and if either of you wants to read about what an unreasonable ignoramus you are, just keep that up. There will be no more of that. Understood?" Both men nodded reluctantly. "Now shake hands," Fran commanded. They did so.

"I will now flip the coin," she announced. "Have either of you got a quarter?"

Monty reached into his pocket and produced a quarter. Fran took it and said, "Heads, we meet in Conference Room A. Tails, B. Ready?"

Art said, "Let me see that coin. It could be a trick."

"Spoken like a sleazy Jew," Monty retorted.

"Enough!" Fran said, raising her voice for the first time. "The coin has a head and a tail."

She tossed it into the air and it fell to the carpet, with George Washington facing up. "Heads," she announced. "Conference Room A."

"A trick," muttered Monty.

Once seated in Conference Room A, Fran opened the meeting. "Gentlemen, we are here to discuss and hopefully resolve an issue that is in the best interests of both of you to resolve. Monty—may I call you Monty?—you have a 10,000 acre parcel of land that is landlocked and therefore of less value than it would be with access. Do you agree?"

"Yes," replied Monty. "That is true."

"And you, Art—may I call you Art?—have a collection of options that would, if exercised, make you the owner of tens of thousands of acres with Monty's parcel in the middle, is that correct?"

Art nodded. "Correct."

"So we are agreed on the situation," Fran said. "I would now like each of you to take a moment and state your positions in civil terms and as objectively as possible. Monty, why don't you go first."

Monty folded his hands and looked solemnly at Fran. "I would rather eat rat poison for a thousand years than sell one square centimeter of land to the Jews. I have sent for settlers to come occupy what heretofore did not seem like home."

"I see," said Fran. "Art, your turn."

Art took a deep breath, saying, "Let there be no doubt that we will get that land. Maybe not tomorrow, but we will make life so miserable for the Arabs that they will beg us to take it."

Fran stood. "Well, gentlemen, sounds like we are close to agreement. Same time next week?"

Chapter 5

Joyce Enlists as Scott Confesses

For the first week after the pit appeared, the Fafalones managed to get by on the one car that had been liberated, George's Lexus, but coordinating the use of that car became increasingly frustrating. George wanted what amounted to exclusive use, and Joyce needed it to shop. On two occasions she offered to drive him to work, but on both days she was late picking him up, which led to arguments and her suggestion that they rent a car. George reminded her of the wolf at the door and the uncertainty of when they could return the rental car given the lack of progress being made on repairs to the pit.

From Joyce's perspective, the only positive in the situation was that it afforded her more time to write letters to Shawn Pen. In fact, she was moving up the chain of command in the Shawn Pen Fan Club. Upon joining several years before, she had been relegated to the status of "member," where all new fans began life in the club. In her first month, she wrote eight fan letters and three checks, which brought her to the attention of the powers that be in the SPFC. After the third check, she received a letter on SPFC letterhead acknowledging her potential, signed in facsimile by Mr. Pen. The letter went on to suggest that continued participation at this level could lead to her being designated as a CP, or "Caring Person." This prospect motivated her to write six more letters and two additional checks, and the day her CP Certificate arrived in the mail was one of celebration. She promptly framed it and set her sights on the next plateau, which was a TCP, "Truly Caring Person."

To reach that goal, she needed to not only maintain her correspondence, both letters and checks, but she was also required to propose at least one worthy cause for consideration by the Shawn Pen Humanitarian International Needs Committee Transmitting Enlightenment & Rectitude (SPHINCTER). After reading in People Magazine that some cities in India were so crowded that families lived on garbage heaps, Joyce proposed that junk automobiles in the U.S. be purchased by SPHINCTER and transported to Mumbai and New Delhi for housing. The letter from SPHINCTER acknowledging receipt of her suggestion praised her global vision without committing the organization, citing certain "logistical considerations" in transporting large amounts of metal across twelve time zones. Still, the letter went on to say, her heart was in the right place, proving that with some additional checks her status might well be elevated to TCP. It was signed in facsimile by Mr. Pen as "Compassionately yours."

It was about this same time that Scott decided

to disclose to Joyce his unusual fixation on women's orthopedic shoes. He found her in the solarium, watching one of her Thai soap operas. She hit the mute button but continued to watch the screen until he said he had something "really important and personal" to tell her. She clicked off the TV, said that if he had come to tell her he was gay he need not stress over the conversation because she had guessed this a long time ago and that a mother's instincts were still the best barometer of a child's nature. He denied being gay, told her that he had been having sex with his girlfriend Allison upstairs since he was fifteen, and that she needed to keep an open mind concerning what she was about to hear.

"Fine," said Joyce, with some hesitation. "My mind is wide open."

"Haven't you noticed I spend a lot of time with shoes?"

"We all spend time with shoes," she said. "Walking around, shopping for them—"

"Mother, stop. I'm weird that way, with shoes. I have this thing . . . this fascination for women's orthopedic shoes. I keep asking if grandmother is coming. I work at a shoe store. I make Allison dress up in them. I volunteer in the geriatrics ward at the hospital. Don't you see a pattern here?"

"Well, now that you mention it."

"I've done some research. It's a fetish, and as fetishes go a harmless one. Still, I don't like it. I'll be going off to college one of these days and I can't afford to let my classmates know I have this problem. I want to be rid of it. Cured. I've signed up for a twelve-step program. It starts next week."

"You mean like the ones the alcoholics use?"

"Yes, like Alcoholics Anonymous. Except they don't have enough people with my problem to fill a meeting, so they lumped a bunch of us together in a group called Miscellaneous Problems Anonymous. Kind of a one size fits all."

"How interesting," said the voice of Joyce.

"We'll see. I'm nervous about it. You have to stand up in the first meeting and confess to the others what your problem is."

"And you're afraid that will embarrass you?"

"I don't know what to call my fetish. Technically, because I have a love of orthopedic shoes, I'm an orthopedophile."

"Oh, that sounds awful."

"See what I mean? No one wants to be a pedophile, even if it has ortho attached. 'Hi, my name's Scott and I'm an orthopedophile.'"

Joyce broke into her proud mother grin. "Whatever you decide to call yourself, I think you are sooooo brave to face this. Your father and I will support you one hundred percent. And I will write to Shawn Pen about it. If you have this problem, there are probably hundreds or thousands who are still in the closet, so to speak. I'll bet this is something that would interest SPHINCTER."

Chapter 6

Kirstin Briefs Fran, Keeping it Brief

A week after soil samples were taken from the pit, Jorge Bustamonte appeared at Fran's door.

"I have very bad news," he said to her. "A core soil sample uncovered the skeletal remains of a ring-tailed scorpion thought to have become extinct. I am afraid we will need to call in an archaeologist and anthropologist to assist."

"Don't tell me Centerfield has an anthropologist on the payroll."

"Of course not. But we have a consulting contract when we need one. She is Esmeralda Bustamonte, a very good woman."

"And a cousin?"

"Married to my cousin."

Fran sighed. "This will take forever, won't it?"

"Not that long. But we have no choice. According to the Preservation of Antiquities Act of 1992, we must investigate."

"Why would anyone want to resurrect dead scorpions? I thought they were lethal. It seems like we would want to wipe them out."

"Of course, and we did," said Jorge. "But it turns out their poison has been shown to cure herpes and has other uses too sensitive to discuss."

"Whatever," said Fran. "I need to get to work. It may be time to investigate putting in another road from a different direction. I need a car."

"I completely understand, but the problem is not easily solved. A new road would require cutting down the mesquite trees, and those are protected as the home of the Wing-Footed Warbler. I will ask Esmeralda to do her work quickly. She is a very good woman."

At the offices of *The Sentinel*, Fran called Kirstin in for their daily briefing. As Kirstin crossed her lanky legs and sipped coffee, Fran was again reminded of what a sophisticated young woman Kirstin was becoming; a young woman with a real future before her. She thought back to their first meeting, when Kirstin's gum-popping immaturity had been on full display. Fran had spoken to her as an adult, and against some long odds Kirstin became one, making a wrenching decision about her pregnancy, jettisoning the tattoo boyfriend, moving back home, and going to school while holding down a job. Fran supposed she was entitled to take some credit for Kirstin's turn around. George and Joyce gave her all the credit, which Fran considered unfair to Kirstin. Change took guts and perseverance, qualities Kirstin had summoned from an untapped wellspring within, while advice took insight and maturity, qualities Fran had acquired in her studies at the University of Life. But it all started with Fran's genuine interest in Kirstin; an interest the girl had perceived from neither George nor Joyce and one she sought desperately in the beds of users and losers. How could Joyce be so wrapped up in do-gooder projects blessed by Shawn Pen when a project named Kirstin greeted her at breakfast every morning? And George, who said he would "give my daughter anything," had failed to give her what she needed most because it didn't come with a price tag and couldn't be parked, docked, flown or worn.

"So," said Fran from behind her desk, "what's new in our town this morning?"

Kirstin consulted her notes. "A strange thing going on at the cemetery," she said. "Two more graves robbed last night. With the three from last week, that makes five. I can't find a report of a single grave robbery in Centerfield's history, so five in two weeks sounds like news."

"It certainly is," Fran said. "This could be a bit awkward since your father owns the cemetery. Have you spoken to him about this?"

"Even though I live there, I interviewed him by phone yesterday. Keeping it professional. He said he is cooperating with the police. Clearly he's resisting the expense required by full time security, but it may come to that."

"Does he have any suspicions about who may be responsible?"

"If he does he didn't share them."

"Weird," Fran said, "but clearly a story. Why does a grave robber go to the trouble? I guess some people want to be buried with valuables—rings or jewelry or who knows what. Keep doing the research and let's run a story next week, assuming you're willing. If you'd rather someone else handle it, I'll understand."

"Nope," said Kirstin, "it's part of my job so I'll do it."

"Good," said Fran. "I like that. Speaking of George, how is he?"

"He talks a lot about losing weight, but he looks for shortcuts. I keep reminding him, 'no pain, no gain, and no loss either.' To tell you the truth, I'm enjoying the chance to lecture him a little. Respectfully, of course, but given the number of lectures I got from him during my lights out days (Kirstin's term for her pre-Fran indulgences), it's nice to score some payback. We're all bummed about the road, but at least we have a car. Dad says he will find a way to get Mom's car across the pit and he mentioned getting your car across, too."

"That's very thoughtful of him. I certainly would be grateful. And your Mom? How is Joyce?"

"She wants a new phone for her birthday, but she has technology issues."

"And Jeff?"

Kirstin grinned. "Jeff is . . . wonderful. We see each other almost every weekend, but just so you know I'm keeping my knees together, as you once advised me to do."

"Excellent," said Fran. "He may be a keeper.

And what is Scott up to these days?"

"Working at the shoe store after school."

"I thought he worked at the hospital."

"That's volunteer. The shoe store is a real job."

"I suppose," said Fran, "but with his special problem it seems a little like an alcoholic tending bar. Does the store sell orthopedic shoes?"

"Special order items, according to Scott. He told me he's looking into a twelve-step program. That seems like a real irony—a twelve-step program to get rid of a shoe fetish."

"I wonder if such a program exists."

"If it does, Scott will find it. He works the internet like a wizard."

A knock on the door interrupted them. It was Ed, who entered dressed for golf. "Are you two working?" he asked. "Someone around here needs to while I work on my putting."

Fran said, "We were just discussing a story about grave robbing. Kirstin tells me there have been five in the last two weeks."

"No kidding," said Ed. "I don't suppose either of you would like to give me a massage before I head to the golf course."

Fran slumped in her chair. "Ed!"

Chapter 7

Ed Meets Elvis

When his friends at the golf course learned that Ed intended to bottle and sell his Barbeque Butter in a nationwide marketing effort, they offered all sorts of advice about how best to do it, most of which he ignored. But one suggestion got his attention. Marv Rawlings, one of his usual foursome and a man with significant manufacturing and production experience with armored vests and other security paraphernalia, told him that his manufacturing costs in China would be one-tenth of what they would be in the U.S. Even Ed knew what that would mean for profits. He questioned Rawlings about the process of finding a manufacturer on the other side of the world.

"Simple as gittin' a pig to roll in mud," Rawlings said. "Them chinks have a guy in Houston. Call him up, tell him what you want to talk about, and he'll not only drive to Centerfield to meet with you but bring take-out and chopsticks with him."

Ed did just that, and one day not long after Mr. Elvis Wu appeared at the offices of *The Sentinel*. He was tall for an Asian, about five-five, with thin, nearly translucent skin, no facial hair, but long sideburns and gelled hair that, through squinting eyes, looked vaguely like you-know-who. Ed greeted him, shook hands, and invited him into conference room A. The aromas of soy-soaked carry-out filled the offices.

"Mr. Wu, you aren't exactly what I was expecting."

Wu chuckled. "Many Americans say that upon first meeting," he said. "You like my hair?"

"And your name," Ed said.

"Not my birth name," Wu offered.

"No kidding," Ed said.

"Chinese name filled with x's and z's. I myself could not pronounce it until I was seven. Came here with parents. Changed name after college."

"Where did you go to school?"

"Virginia Tech. Many Elvis fans there. Forty-three trips to Graceland so far."

"My buddy Marv tells me you're a fine businessman, and we admire that here in Texas. Tell me about your company."

"I start company eight years ago. Veddy solid balance sheet. No debt. We doing well."

"Good to hear," Ed said. "Exactly what do you do?"

"Mostly we take jobs from Americans and move them to China."

Ed cleared his throat. "That's an odd sales pitch, Mr. Wu. As an American and a Texan, I want to keep jobs here so we can grow our economy and maintain our way of life."

Wu smiled as he offered Ed sushi. "No chance. Too late for that, Mr. Ed. American companies have too many chefs, no Indians."

"You mean chiefs?"

"Yes, chiefs. Too many chiefs. In China every man does work of five men and get small pay. In America five chiefs do work of one man and get big bonus. You fucked."

Ed rubbed his chin as a grudging admission that Wu had a point. "Look, Mr. Wu, I need someone somewhere to make and bottle my product: Ed's Barbeque Butter. I got a bottle of it with me now. Want to taste it?" He handed the bottle to Wu.

Wu studied the label, unscrewed the cap, and put his nose over the mouth of the bottle. "Yum," he said. "Smells good. I try on fried rice." He opened one of the take-out cartons and poured the liquid in. With chopsticks he lifted rice and butter to his lips. He chewed slowly, then took another bite. "Must have this," he said. "New sauce for fried rice."

Ed said, "Now look, Wu, this here is barbeque sauce, a thing I know quite a bit about. There will be high demand for it here in Texas and everywhere great barbeque is worshipped. I intend to make selling it my life's work. So let's talk turkey, as we say. How much would it cost me to make one thousand bottles of it in China?"

Wu glanced toward the ceiling. "One . . . thousand . . . bottles? About forty dollars."

Ed's jaw dropped. "Forty dollars?"

"What, too high? Okay, thirty-five."

"You don't even know what's in it."

Wu flapped his hand dismissively. "Does not matter. Thirty-five. Final offer."

So Ed signed a contract with Wu's company for one thousand bottles to test market in the U.S. and gave Wu a twenty-dollar deposit. He also took the precaution of having Rick Lopez prepare a non-disclosure agreement, which Wu signed before receiving the formula.

One month later, UPS delivered a test batch labeled "Mr Ed Buttered Butter" to the offices of *The Sentinel*. Ed shook his head at the mangled trademark, wondering if the product he was about to sample had likewise been mangled. He unscrewed the top, poured out some on his finger, and tasted. He replaced the top and called Elvis Wu.

"Say, Wu, I just tried the stuff you had sent from China. Call me crazy but it tastes like motor oil."

"Mix-up at plant," Wu said. "Your label put on wrong container. Quaker State not happy either. Drivers getting oil change with barbeque sauce."

"Sounds like a pretty sloppy operation you got going on over there. Maybe we just forget the whole thing."

"No, Mr. Ed. We do better. One more chance. We veddy organized." Then Wu invited Ed to China to see the plant.

Ed thanked him for the invitation, realizing as he did so that there was something about Wu he liked. Maybe it was his entrepreneurial spirit, reminding Ed of what Texas had been in the days his father founded the newspaper, when wildcatters lived for months on grits and hope, drilling on a gambler's instinct for that dark, crude, viscous vein that, when hit, turned a cowboy into a king.

"Elvis? May I call you Elvis?"

"I would be honored, Mr. Ed."

"Elvis, I'm going to tell you the Texas truth, and there is no truth truer than the Texas truth except when we bullshit women, which we do with some regularity. The idea of spending thirty hours on an airplane to get to a place where they eat funny food, practice some weird customs and don't speak English is not my idea of time well spent. I can get all that in New York with lots less travel."

"I understand, Mr. Ed, so I see no need to tell you of beautiful Chinese women who would bring disgrace upon the family unless they granted your every desire and answered every question."

Suddenly, Ed had lots of questions.

Chapter 8

*George Weighs in as
his Doctor Cops Out*

George dreaded his annual physical, but his close call with the heart attack sobered him enough to keep his appointment with Dr. Malloy. He liked Dr. Malloy's "old school" bedside manner, perfected during the doctor's days at an old school in Connecticut. What George particularly appreciated was the doctor's way of making him feel better about things that otherwise may have been cause for concern.

Like his blood pressure: 210 over 120. Dr. Malloy described this as "modestly elevated" while Doctor Tan, his heart surgeon and a much younger man than Dr. Malloy, who was 78, had called it "a cheeseburger away from coronary infarction." Or his weight. George liked the old scales that used to be employed, when the nurse simply noted in his chart "above 250." But a Medicare audit had written Dr. Malloy up for this, insisting that close enough was a violation of government regulations, quoting eight Medicare bulletins on the subject. So many of Dr. Malloy's patients now maxed out the traditional scales that he was forced to purchase, at a cost of twelve thousand dollars, a new industrial one traditionally sold to meat packing companies for precise measurement of slabs of beef between three hundred and fifteen hundred pounds. George approached the new scales with the look of a French nobleman being led to the guillotine. He stepped up onto the ample platform, held his breath, closed his eyes, and waited. The nurse, eying the digital readout, reported 338.

"Wait," George said. "I forgot to take off my shoes."

When George and Dr. Malloy were alone in the consultation room, the doctor noted that for a man with an admittedly large frame, George seemed a "tad on the heavy side" and suggested a "moderate diet of more fruits and vegetables."

After reminding Dr. Malloy that his weight included his shoes, George said, "Doc, those diets just don't work for me. I've tried them all. I need something quicker and easier. Isn't there a pill? I thought I read that someplace."

Dr. Malloy twisted the end of his white handlebar moustache and studied the ceiling. "Well . . . there is always liposuction. I don't like recommending it to my patients unless they are what I consider morbidly obese."

"And I'm not there."

"Certainly not," agreed the doctor. "But close."

"Is liposuction expensive?"

"Very, but your insurance should cover most of it provided it is deemed medically necessary, which usually means morbidly obese."

"How far away am I?"

"About 22 pounds. A little more now than I know you were weighed with your shoes on."

"Are you telling me I need to gain weight?"

"Only if you want insurance coverage. If you're prepared to write a check we could schedule it tomorrow."

"So if I gain, say, twenty-five pounds, I save . . ."

"Seventy-five thousand dollars. More if you need aspirin."

"Doc, I'm going to dedicate myself to those twenty-five pounds. Consider them gained."

"That's the spirit. Try to do it slowly. Avoid fruits and vegetables. Now, what other problems have you been experiencing?"

"My knees are killing me. Getting in and out of the golf cart is becoming painful."

"A common complaint as we age. Let me give you a prescription for pain that many of my patients have become fond of."

"Is it addictive?"

"Only if taken in the quantities I prescribe. Try to have a little left over at the end of the month. You should be fine. Anything else besides those knees?"

George looked around in conspiratorial circumspection. "Well, there is a little issue with my willie, if you get my drift."

"Your . . .willie?"

"You know, my schlong, my prick. It's dead."

"Ah," said Dr. Malloy, nodding. "Erectile dysfunction."

"Yeah. I can't get it up, and if I get it up it doesn't stay up. I play reveille and it hears taps. I need that—"

"Little blue pill," the doctor said with a grin. "Marvelous contribution to modern medicine. I'll write you a prescription. Anything else?"

"I guess that's it. Are we done?

"One last procedure before we finish." Dr. Malloy rose from the stool on which he had been seated and from a drawer extracted a rubber glove. "I guess you know the one I mean. Please drop your drawers and bend over the gurney."

"I hate this," said George.

Dr. Malloy coated his middle finger with KY jelly as he approached George's ample, now-bear posterior. "I have a colleague, a proctologist, who calls it the 'Vaseline rocket in the butt cheeks' pocket,' but I find that undignified, don't you?"

Chapter 9

George Follows Doctor's Orders

George returned from his physical with a spring in his step. Not only had Dr. Malloy accepted without question or comment George's lies about his drinking habits ("An occasional glass of wine with dinner"), but he had actually ordered George to gain weight. For once he didn't mutter curses at having to park at the edge of the pit and walk around. He whistled as he walked through the mesquite trees and the security fence and entered his home.

"How did it go, dear?" Joyce asked.

"Never better. Doc Malloy told me to gain some weight."

"Did he now? That's a bit of a surprise."

"I need to put on about twenty-five pounds so the insurance company will pay for liposuction. Hey, let's go out to dinner to celebrate."

"I'd love that," said Joyce. "Where should be go?"

"I hear good things about that new chain, the Golden Glop. Order the Maneater everyone says. Let's give it a try."

Things were booming at the Golden Glop when they arrived, with the aroma of fresh grease in the air. A very thin hostess who looked like she might be fifteen showed them to a table by a large plate glass window. On the table rested a bottle of catsup, salt and pepper, and Holy Moly hot sauce. A small vase held a lone plastic flower. The hostess handed them each a menu and left.

A waitress approached with glasses of ice water. If her name tag could be believed, her name was Lindsey and she was about as a wide as she was tall, with a bad complexion to round out the image. She was chewing gum. Joyce told her this was a celebration and asked that a candle be brought for the table. Lindsey looked annoyed and said she wasn't sure they had candles and that her boss had said something about the risk of grease fires.

Joyce asked, "How is the fish?"

"Disgusting," Lindsey replied. "I hate fish."

"I see," said Joyce. "And the chicken?"

"I had that last week," Lindsey said. "Barfed my guts out. Missed two days of work. I don't think they use real chicken."

"Then perhaps I'll have just a nice soup and salad," Joyce said. "How is the minestrone?"

"Pig swill," said Lindsey. "I'd avoid that. Tomato is really not that bad when it's hot."

"Tomato it is, then. With the garden salad."

"Can't go wrong there," Lindsey said as she noted the order on her pad, then turned to George.

"No salad for this Jose," he said. "I'll have a triple bourbon on the rocks, the double-dipped onion rings, and the Maneater. I hear it's real meat for a real man."

"And real big," Lindsey acknowledged.

"And a bottle of wine," George added. "That merlot stuff."

As they waited for their food, Joyce reached across the table to take George's hand. "You know," she said coyly, "your little pop tart has a birthday coming up."

"Oh yeah," he said. "Is it next month?"

"It's next week, silly. Want to know what I want?"

"Do tell."

"The new IDrone. It has so many features I can't believe it."

"You have a phone," George said. "It works great. Why do you need an IDrone? Those things cost big money."

"Now, George, you're very successful and we can afford it. And the IDrone has something no other phone has."

"And that would be . . . ?"

Joyce paused dramatically, then turned her head up, as if expecting a heavenly visitation. "That would be the new application—I think it's called an 'app'—that the Shawn Pen Fan Club has put out. It only runs on the IDrone. With it I can submit ideas directly to SPHINCTER. Ideas that can change the world."

"Yeah," George groused, "and maybe we should buy an IDrone for the wolf at the door while we're at it. I don't know, Joyce. Your history with things that have on-off switches isn't the best. You just now learned the phone you have. Are you sure you want something new and complicated?"

"Very sure, dear."

The food arrived. George dove into the Maneater with relish. Joyce lifted her fork over her salad, then said to Lindsey, "I've never seen fried lettuce."

"Specialty of the house," she said. "Bon appetite."

Chapter 10

Buster the Mayor

Fran was ten minutes early for her appointment with the mayor. For some time she had been concerned about haphazard development in Centerfield, particularly as that development threatened to swallow some of the last large tracts of land that could one day serve as the park Fran and others envisioned. She had been in a number of meetings and receptions with Buster since his election as mayor, but she wanted this private conference to find out where he stood on the park.

She approached the reception desk and stated to the woman seated at the computer terminal, Rosalinda Bustamonte, her name and that she was here for her appointment with Mayor Buster. Everyone called him Mayor Buster. The woman looked at her with an uncomprehending stare. At that moment, another woman from a nearby desk appeared at Fran's elbow.

"She can't understand you. She's just learning English. But doing very well. May I be of assistance?"

Fran shifted her gaze between the two women. "She's the mayor's receptionist and she doesn't speak English?"

"Yet. She's working hard at it. She's wonderful with our Spanish speaking citizens." Here, the woman lowered her voice. "And, she's the mayor's sister."

"I see," said Fran, making mental note to inquire into what the town was paying Rosalinda to communicate with roughly twenty percent of the population. "Well, if you could tell the mayor I'm here for our three o'clock appointment."

"Of course," the English speaker said pleasantly. "Just follow me."

Fran was ushered into Buster's spacious office. He was on the phone but motioned for her to sit down.

"Yes, yes," Buster said to the caller. "I understand how important it is, and I will not let down you or the other members of the El Paso Buster Booster Club. How many bezzballs should I bring? Yes, good, alright. See you next Monday." He hung up, stood, walked around his desk and shook Fran's hand.

"Ah," he said. "My worthy opponent. To tell the truth, Fran, there are many days when I wish you had won. This job is thankless work. But I am glad you are here. This is your first visit to my office, is it not?

"Yes."

"Then let me show you my MVP trophy over here. Most players who win it must decide whether to display it at home or at work, but since I won two, I don't have to choose. And here is a photograph of me giving my acceptance speech at the Hall of Fame in Canton, Ohio."

"I'm from Ohio," noted Fran.

"They have good bezzball teams in Ohio, but the Cubs are not one of them."

"The Cubs are also not in Ohio," she injected. "That would be Illinois."

"You are certain?"

"I'm positive the Chicago Cubs play in Illinois, yes."

"To someone from Mexico it is hard to keep it all straight. This country, that used to be my country before your army beat my army, and that is now my country because I came here and made your country my country, is so large and spread out. You have heard of Acapulco?"

Fran looked puzzled. "I believe most Americans have heard of Acapulco."

Buster nodded decisively. "And do you know what Mexican state Acapulco is in?"

"I confess I haven't the faintest idea."

"I do not think one in a hundred Americans know the answer. That lack of interest in Mexico's geography and history is a subject of much resentment there. But you did not come to hear such things. What brings *The Sentinel's* editor to see me today?"

Fran stated her concerns about the park. "At the rate developers are gobbling up land, there will soon be no tract big enough for a park, which is vital to Centerfield's future."

"How much land do you think will be required?"

"Possibly as much as one hundred acres."

"That is a big park," Buster said. "Much bigger than the parks I played in."

"Well, those were baseball parks and the needs of regular people are a bit different. We need picnic areas, bike trails, soccer fields, and lots of woods for wildlife."

"I myself was a big fan of wildlife in my youth, but now I am older and prefer quiet evenings at home. This park; it will be expensive?"

"There will be some expense, of course. How much will be dictated by the design. I believe I can talk the paper into funding a significant portion of the architectural fees."

"That is quite generous. The paper is a good citizen. When the time comes to select the architects, we should keep in mind Cardenez & Bustamonte, LLP. It is a very good firm."

Fran retained her poker face. "Of course, all qualified firms should be considered. I'm sure your cousin's firm does excellent work."

"No. Cardenez is not my cousin."

"I meant Bustmonte."

"Yes, he is my cousin."

"So," said Fran, taking a deep breath, "back to the original point, which was how to keep developers from buying up all the available land. If Centerfield has to later buy it back from them it will bankrupt the town."

"We cannot allow that to happen," Buster said, his brow furrowing in concern. "Bankruptcy would be bad, and remember my campaign promise . . . good things, si—"

"I know, I know, don't remind me," Fran said. "Good things, si, bad things, no."

"Exactly. And since bankruptcy would be a bad thing, we must not allow it. I think the park would be a good thing, yes?"

"Very good. So how do we stop the developers?"

Buster shook his head from side to side several times. "That is a big problem, because this is Texas and we have the great tradition of letting developers do whatever they want. Many of them are friends of mine. They buy big skyboxes for bezzball. I think we should leave them alone."

Fran had an idea. "When I mentioned the picnic areas and the soccer fields and the other things that would go into the park, did I mention the statue?"

"No. You said nothing about a statue."

"I can't believe I didn't mention it. Every public park has a statue. You know, someone who is considered a hero by the town."

A gleam came into Buster's eyes. "This would be a large statue?"

"Very large," Fran said. "To be seen by everyone from a great distance."

"And who would be this hero?"

"I can only guess that some prominent citizen, like a mayor, would be considered."

Buster brought his well-manicured hand down flat on the table. "You are right about this park. We need this park. This park would be good. I will see what I can do."

"Excellent," Fran said, standing to leave. Then, she hesitated. "Oh, one more thing," she said. "I suppose you've heard about the hole in my street."

"Yes. That is bad."

"Correct. A large pit in a residential street is bad. And dangerous. And it's been there for a month. Can you see what can be done to get it repaired?"

"But of course. We will put our best people on it. A large hole in the street is bad, and you know what I say, good things . . ."

Fran blocked it out, wondering how much money she would need to challenge Buster in the next election. She stood, extended her hand, and thanked the mayor for his time. He walked her to the door. As she was leaving he called to her.

"Guerrero," he said. "Acapulco is in the state of Guerrero."

"I'll remember that." And she meant it.

Chapter 11

Art Leers as Tricksy gets in Shape

Art could hear the music from the driveway. He entered the house and walked straight to the den, where Tricksy was in the splits position on the carpet. She wore last summer's bikini; pink top, blue bottom, with a sedate little bow on each hip, so sweet it could have passed for a child's swimsuit. In fact, it was a child's swimsuit. Tricksy liked the way it accentuated her assets. Art liked that, too.

"Hey there, sugar," she said over the music, a Donna Summer disco fever number. "I'm almost finished for today. Then I'll rustle us up some dinner."

"Take your time," Art said, sinking into the couch to admire the view.

She pumped out twenty push-ups, then stood and turned off the music, patting her forehead with a towel. "That's hard work," she said, "but I'm getting in shape."

"When do I get to watch you work?"

She pinched skin at her waist. "As soon as I get rid of this," she said. "I want you to see me at my best."

"You are perfect now," Art said.

"And you are just the biggest love in Texas for

saying such a sweet thing."

"Do you know Mike at Murphy's Muffler?"

A momentary panic flashed over Tricksy's face, but she recovered while Art was looking at her legs. "Sure, I know Mike. Went to high school with him. Why?"

"No reason. I told him you had taken an evening job at The North Pole and he said he was surprised. What is a fall chicken?"

"Beats me."

"He said he was surprised because you are not a fall chicken."

Tricksy's eyes narrowed. "Are you sure he didn't say spring chicken?"

"Spring chicken? Yes, he did say spring chicken."

"That's an expression that means I'm getting older. Well, who isn't? I'd like to tell that Mike where he can put his monkey wrench."

"Where?"

"Never mind, dear. It is true that most of the girls . . . ladies that work at The North Pole are younger, but I have something they don't have: experience. And half the time they won't show up because they stay out all night to party. I'm dependable and hardworking. That is the way to get ahead. Besides, that four hundred dollars I brought home last Friday came in handy, did it not?"

"A true blessing," Art agreed. "Do all Christmas shoppers pay in cash?"

"No, that's the North Pole's system. I think you'll understand it better when you see me work."

"I hope that will be soon."

She walked to the couch, leaned down, and kissed him full on the lips. "It will be, or my name isn't Sue Collins."

"But your name isn't Sue Collins."

"For a few hours a week, it is. Now let's see what we can find for dinner. Working out always makes me hungry."

Chapter 12

An Aging Pit welcomes
New Faces

Benny returned to the pit with the same crane he had used to lift George's car from the edge weeks before. Fran couldn't afford the service, but neither could she afford to be without a car any longer. She drove her car to the edge, where Benny's crane lifted it skyward before lowering it onto what had now become the neighborhood parking lot just outside Fran's yard. No one on Hobbit Lane liked the arrangement except Scott, who was making some serious money washing cars. Mutterings about the pit escalated daily, fueled by the lack of repair activity. Ring tailed scorpions became the target of venomous oaths.

One day a paneled truck pulled up to the pit and a buzz went through the neighborhood that help had finally arrived. Those hopes were immediately dashed when a tall man with a trimmed beard emerged from the driver's seat. He wore a faded Bruce Hornsby tee shirt and cargo shorts--hardly dressed for road repair. From the passenger side came a young woman who appeared to be college age, and when the van door opened more young people climbed out. The driver began giving directions for the unloading of ladders and tarps.

Soon, ladders extended into the pit, where the half-dozen young people began spreading tarps.

Fran, home for lunch, walked out to investigate. She approached the driver, who wore wire-rim glasses revealing clear blue eyes. "I'm just guessing your name is Bustamonte," she said.

"I beg your pardon?" he said. "My name is Roger McCall."

"Then you must be married to a Bustamonte."

"I'm not married to anyone. And you are . . . ?"

"Sorry," she said, extending her hand. "I'm Fran. That's my house you parked in front of. We have a little nepotism issue going on in Centerfield and I just assumed you were more of the same."

"I'm from Texas State," said Roger, who looked to be about thirty-five. "San Marcos campus. These are some of my archaeology students. We're here to explore the pottery shards they found in the soil samples. Didn't they tell you we were coming?"

Fran looked down, shook her head slowly from side to side, and answered, "They did not. How long will this take?"

"Depends on what we find. If it's just Clovis era stuff, we'll probably be gone in a few days. There's plenty of that around, so we don't need more, but the shards found appear to date from about 15,000 years back, so that predates Clovis. Could be important."

"And if it turns out to be pre-Clovis?"

McCall rubbed his chin. "My guess is we'll still be digging when I retire. Well, time to get to work."

Fran watched him walk away toward one of the ladders now extending into the pit. He was lean and muscled, with tanned and well-defined calves. She resolved to bring lemonade.

Chapter 13

Monty Lures Halim
to Centerfield

Mamoud Abbar, a/k/a Monty Archer, placed a call to his old friend Aamil, who lived with his family of seven in a one-bedroom apartment in the Gaza Strip. They lived hand to mouth, day to day, their sole luxuries consisting of a cell phone and cable TV, which allowed them to watch soap operas produced in Turkey. Monty described to his friend the situation and the critical importance of bringing Arabs to live in New Palestine. He made an impassioned plea for Aamil to bring his family to Texas to help make a last stand against Israeli hegemony. He mentioned Davy Crockett and the Alamo.

Aamil listened patiently before replying. "My dear friend," he said. "You have been in America too long, or you have been in the Texas sun too long. There are several things standing in our way of joining you. First, we are not allowed to leave Gaza, much less what passes for Old Palestine. Second, if we could leave, there is no source of visas for travel. Who would return here if they ever got out? Lastly, such travel would cost thousands of dollars and we have only the equivalence of $9. My cell service may be interrupted before this call is ended because I am behind on my bill."

"So there is no work?"

"Not since 1999, and that is a long time without a paycheck."

"How do you spend your time?"

"We watch TV and we go to rallies in the street. They serve free food at rallies."

"I see," said Monty. "And there is no way to raise money?"

"Only one. Hummus will pay me to blow myself up."

"Does that pay well?"

"Oh, very well. The minimum guarantee is $3000 U.S., but there is a points system that can make my family rich. Bonus points are awarded for every casualty, and that is in addition to the location bonus. Anyone can strap on the exploding vest and walk into the marketplace, but a bus during rush hour or a mosque during services is very lucrative. I'm considering it. Listen, old friend. Everyone here is in the same cave as me. We have no money, no way out, and no hope. If I were you, I would recruit people who are already in America. Run an ad in the Arab newspaper in Detroit. Advertise free land. That should bring some of our people to Texas."

"Your advice is very sound," Monty said. "I will follow it. And do not blow yourself up. Your family would miss you and I would miss you."

"That is very kind. My oldest son is a very smart boy. With money I could send him to school.

That is the only reason I would consider such a drastic measure. I wish you great fortune in your effort to populate New P. Perhaps someday I can come visit you there."

Monty ran a classified that appeared in the Sunday edition of Al Gae (literally, "a one-cell source for news"), the Arabic language newspaper in Detroit. It read as follows: "Tired of the mean streets of Detroit? Weary of crime, smog, and losing professional sports franchises? Come to Texas, where every family will be awarded a free acre of land as long as the supply lasts. For more information call Monty."

Results were immediate. Monty took a call from one Halim, who identified himself as an unemployed cab driver. "Excellent," Monty said. "There are currently no cab drivers in New P, so you would have the business all to yourself."

"Would it take me long to learn the streets?"

"Not at all," Monty answered honestly. "Are you married?"

"Yes, with two children. My wife is a waitress."

"This is very good. I often have said that what New P needs is a well-trained waitress. She will be welcome."

"The ad says a free acre of land. It seems too good to be true."

"I too would be skeptical, but believe me when I say it is the absolute truth. Within twenty-four hours of your arrival and confirmation that you are, in fact, Arabs, a deed from the Porkrind Trust will be recorded in your name."

"And the schools?"

Monty hesitated. "The schools? Think of them as the equivalent of Montessori. The children learn what interests them at their own pace. Very unstructured."

Halim promised to arrive in ten days. When he called from St. Louis to confirm the family was on its way, Monty knew New P was not technically ready for permanent residents, lacking as it did a single road, a house, water, sewer, stores, a school, a restaurant, metered parking, speed bumps, a no litter zone, and any other accoutrement of civilization. Further, and perhaps more significantly, Monty knew that Halim did not realize this, since the only question he focused on concerned the promised acre of land. Perhaps, Monty reasoned, people with a chance to leave Detroit didn't ask questions. But while the element of surprise is an asset in war, it is decidedly not an asset when welcoming a family of four that has just driven thousands of miles to begin life in Texas. Monty wanted to make Halim happy, because only in that way would Halim be motivated to call friends back in Detroit to report the wonderful opportunities that awaited them in Texas.

Monty instructed Halim to meet him in front of City Hall, and from there they would caravan to the property. At more or less the agreed upon time, Monty spotted a rusty, dusty purple van dappled with bondo and with Michigan tags pass slowly by his parked pick-up. Monty sounded the horn, the van stopped, and Halim emerged from the driver's seat, followed by Hessa, his wife, Najair, his son, and Rayya, his daughter. The children looked to be about eight and six, respectively.

"Welcome to Centerfield," Monty said, spreading his arms in metaphorical embrace.

"This looks very nice," said Halim. "It looks nothing like Detroit. Is the land far?"

"Outside of town," Monty said. "About twenty-five miles."

"I notice," said Halim, "that your truck is pulling a house trailer."

"Yes, well technically speaking there are no houses yet in New P, so I brought along a place for you to live."

"How thoughtful," said Hessa, who had pretty brown eyes set in an oval face, her head covered by a hijab.

"Is there a baseball team?" asked Najair.

"No, but there is a famous baseball player. His name is Buster Bustamonte and he's in the Hall of Fame. He is also our mayor."

"Can I meet him?" asked Najair, wide-eyed.

"Of course you can meet him," replied Monty, relieved to be able to fulfill at least one expectation. "Let's get started. We want to arrive in New P while the sun is shining."

An hour later they stopped at what Monty

remembered as the edge of New P's ten thousand acres. He got out, approached Halim's van, and said, "Here we are. New Palestine. You will be very happy here."

Monty watched as the family surveyed the endless, unbroken stretch of prairie before them. "It is not very crowded," Halim said.

"Technically, you are the first family here. Pioneers. But soon others will follow."

"Where is our acre of land?" Hessa asked.

"Anywhere you want it to be," Monty replied.

"You mean we can choose any acre in the entire country?" Halim asked.

"Take your pick," said Monty. "Would you prefer to be in the center of town, where the action is, or nearer the edge, where it is peaceful."

Halim looked at Hessa and they said, simultaneously, "the center."

"Excellent decision," said Monty. "Today the center looks very much like the edge, but one day you will be in the middle of a vibrant town."

"What about the neighbors?" Hessa asked. "Are they farmers?"

"Not exactly," said Monty. Then, unable to repress the thought, he muttered, "Keep your children and the sheep away from them. But don't worry, you probably won't run into them."

Monty drove to what he guessed was more or less the center of the tract. In fact, he hadn't set foot on the property in many years and had only a vague of New P's boundaries. "How is this?" he asked. "Nice view, level surface, centrally located. It's perfect if you ask me."

"Is that a creek?" asked Hessa, pointing to a nearby fissure in the earth.

"During flash floods, yes," said Monty.

Chapter 14

Fran Uses her Editorial Bark for a Park

Fran's meeting with Buster whetted her editorial appetite as few things in recent memory had done. The idea that no restrictions could be placed on developers because many of the them bought skyboxes for "beezball" was absurd on its face, and getting something done before it was too late challenged her. She summoned Kirstin.

"We need to know where we stand. How many hundred-acre tracts are left in Centerfield, where are they, who owns them, and what controls if any does the city code place on developing them? Go see Tricksy at the courthouse. She should be able to point you to the records you need to answer three of those four questions. I'll have Rick Lopez research the city code issue."

"In other words," said Kirstin, taking notes, "as far as the park is concerned we need to know whether we're in the seventh, eighth or ninth inning."

"Please," pleaded Fran, "I know you mean well, but let's leave the baseball metaphors alone."

"Sure," said Kirstin, a bit hurt.

One week later, Fran had her answers. Kirstin had gone the extra mile by printing a map of the city and color-coding the four qualifying parcels. Two were already owned by developers, one was tied up in an estate, and the fourth, by location the most desirable, was owned by Amos Albright.

The legend of Amos Albright was well known in Centerfield; ironic in that few, including Fran, knew him at all and none knew him well. Reclusive, enigmatic, and just plain odd were the adjectives most often used to describe him. What information was known came from a distant cousin tracked down by a reporter for the Houston Chronicle for a story on that cousin's grandfather, an oil baron who had died intestate, triggering a fifty-state search for possible heirs, of which Amos Albright may have been one. According to the source, one Eugene "Flippo" Laurens, Cousin Amos left home at sixteen to join the circus, drawn by his fascination for the exotic animals. He tended the animals for the next several years and saw much of the country as the circus moved by train, mostly in the South and West. When one of the regular clowns broke a leg, the owner pressed Albright into service despite his protests. Not only did he have none of the skills needed to clown, but he worried that his animals would suffer neglect at the hands of inexperienced caretakers. But one fact above all others repelled Albright from the new job: he was utterly humorless, and he knew it. Whether he regretted this personality trait was unknown, but none who came into contact with him doubted its truth. Circus folk speculated that his humor deficiency accounted for his love of the elephants, tigers and the lone giraffe. They took him for what he was and never demanded to be entertained, only fed and well cared for.

It therefore came as quite a shock to the circus colony that Amos excelled as a clown, and no one was more surprised than Amos himself. He told Flippo Laurens, during a stopover in Wichita, that he figured it was the outfit and the makeup. The disguise allowed him to be someone he was not. For the first time in his life, Amos made people laugh, and so intoxicated did he become by doing so that he spent the rest of his circus career in the same face paint he learned in his first day on the job.

But cavorting as a clown, to the delight of children, parents and grandparents, did not translate into a robust social life for Amos, or any at all. Circus personnel couldn't recall seeing him on a date, in a bar, or at a dance. He stayed in his trailer, reading and listening to music on a small transistor radio. He saved his paychecks relentlessly, and because those who worked with him never saw him spend any money, it was accepted lore that he had flush bank accounts in the cities hosting the circus. He retired on the day he became eligible for Social Security and, for reasons neither known nor explained, moved to Centerfield.

He did not hoard his money in banks, as commonly thought, but instead bought real estate, in Centerfield and other small communities, mostly in Texas and Oklahoma. Judging by public records, his investment philosophy was simplicity itself--buy selectively and never, ever sell. His holdings in and around Centerfield totaled almost eight hundred acres, the largest being the site identified by Kirstin.

"They say he's weird," Kirstin said as Fran studied her map.

"Who?" Fran asked absently.

"That Amos Albright. Have you ever seen him?"

"I met him once. It may have been at some animal rights rally; I can't remember exactly. Do you have an address for him?"

Kirstin, anticipating the request, handed her a note. "What's the word from Lawyer Rick?"

"The city could enact some zoning restrictions that would make these tracts less attractive for development. That said, the idea that people can't do with their property what they want doesn't fly very high or far here in Texas. I think it's time for an editorial."

Two days later, this appeared on *The Sentinel's* editorial page.

If there is a single place that defines a town, that in the body politic can be said to be the heart and soul of its citizens, it is a public park. Properly designed and constructed, a public park serves as the community water cooler, its communal picnic, its collective back yard for things like soccer and baseball, and its flower garden for Nature's seasonal displays of color. Parks remind us of who we are, and Centerfield doesn't have one. Worse yet, unless the mayor and our elected officials move quickly, we may never have the kind of park that our community deserves.

Why is this true? Because the choicest land is

being acquired and developed by those for whom a park is just another amenity, and because experience confirms that when profits collide with the public good, the public good usually finishes second.

The Sentinel acknowledges the entrepreneurial spirit that has made Centerfield what it is today. Without it, we wouldn't live in such a vibrant, progressive place. Our businesses large and small are good corporate citizens, and that includes some of the very developers who could make this park a reality. Without the tax base those businesses provide, without their leaders who contribute their time and money to our boards, commissions and charities, our town would be a much less desirable place. And lest it be forgotten, not only is this newspaper not anti-business, but we are ourselves a business.

One legitimate function of government is to sensibly regulate the growing pains every community like ours experiences. It is hoped a developer, or perhaps a public-private partnership, will step forward to spearhead the public park initiative. Failing that, the mayor and elected representatives must take the lead by acquiring sufficient land before it is all gone. The future of Centerfield depends upon it.

Chapter 15

Kirstin and Jeff talk things over

Kirstin and Jeff saw each other almost every weekend. Usually, he made the trip from Houston to Centerfield. It had not been easy for her to confide her early sexual promiscuity, but she had employed lessons learned from Fran to be candid. He replied with some confessions of his own, insisting he realized a double standard was at work in Centerfield and elsewhere. She liked that. She told him she was "wild" about him but wouldn't sleep with him so not to ask. He said he understood and would honor her request, but couldn't help thinking about it. "No more than I do," she said, and kissed him on the lips.

As she left *The Sentinel's* offices one afternoon, she thought she saw her old tattoo boyfriend Pete slumped down in a car parked across the lot. Not again, she thought, and mentioned it to Jeff.

"Bad news there, love," he said. "His parole ended last week. Unless he does something overt, there isn't much we can do. Public parking lot, free country, all that."

"Something overt like raping and strangling me?"

"I'll talk to an attorney buddy of mine about the stalking law. Hopefully, that will help."

She reached for his hand. "I'm not worried as

long as I have my bouncer with me."

"I can't say I blame him for not wanting to let go," Jeff said.

"You're sweet, but he's just stubborn, and obsessed, and a little crazy. Changing subjects, I'd like you to come with me on this grave robbing story. We've had a recent rash of them."

"So I read in the paper."

She smiled. "Now why would a parole officer in Houston read the little old *Sentinel*?"

"I love the sports coverage," he said, winking. "Where are we going to learn who is robbing graves?"

"I figure we'll start with the pawn shops. My dad gave me an inventory of sorts. Some people want to be buried with their jewelry."

"But how would a grave robber know that unless he was a member of the family or close friend?"

"Or maybe had inside information from someone who works for my dad. But two of the graves robbed contained no jewelry, so either the thieves rob randomly . . ."

"Or they are after something else," Jeff said. "Can you reuse a casket?"

"I wondered about that," she said, grabbing her purse and car keys. "I'd like to think my dad wouldn't knowingly participate in something like that, but maybe in other places they wouldn't notice or care."

"What about the bodies themselves? The cadavers."

The Moralist II

She gave a quick grin. "I need to check EBay to see what kind of bids skeletons are bringing. Ready?"

Chapter 16

Joyce Beams as George Despairs

When George surprised Joyce with an IDrone for her birthday, she wasn't the least bit surprised, having provided him with a detailed description of the color and features she wanted. He grumbled about the wolf at the door. And despite the fact that she herself had picked it up from the IDrone store and wrapped it with a note that read "To Joyce with love, George," she did a little jig of happiness when she opened it.

She searched the box for instructions, then realized they were on the IDrone, which she struggled to turn on but eventually succeeded. From a desk drawer she removed the instructions from SPHINCTER for downloading its application. "Oh, this is sooooo exciting," she crooned, staring at the screen as if, in moments, Shawn Pen himself would appear on her screen, and in fact he did.

"Hello, Truly Caring Person," Shawn Pen said. "And thank you for downloading this world-saving application. Together, we will do great things for people in faraway lands even though things are a mess here in the United States. By embracing this technology, you and thousands of others can quickly and easily fund such projects as TAMP, "Teaching Africans to Make Pasta." Tragically, some in Africa live on only pennies a year, so cannot afford expensive food or even first run movies. I want to assure you that over eleven percent of the $299 cost of this application will go directly into caring."

George, seated next to her, coughed. "The _app_ cost $299?"

Joyce shushed him. "People are starving, George. It is the least we can do. Now, let Shawn finish."

"So make TAMP your project like it is mine," Pen intoned, "and together we will TAMP on until the work is done." His image slowly dissolved.

Joyce was close to tears. "I'm with you, Shawn," she managed to say.

"How close are we to dinner?" George asked.

"I can't think about that now," she said. "I'm too excited. And look at all these other applications I can download. Here is one that allows you to turn off your ice maker from anywhere in the world."

"Now why would anyone want to turn off an ice maker? Does it cost $299, because if it does you can forget it."

"No, silly, it's free. Hundreds of them are free. Here's one to help us name our pet."

"I can't help but notice that our cat already has a name."

She tapped her fingernail on an icon. "And this one tells you when shrimp are cooked. I always get that wrong."

"I have a bad feeling about this," George said.

Chapter 17

Scott Takes Step 1 of 12

Scott dreaded his first meeting of Miscellaneous Problems Anonymous, but he was firm in his resolve to overcome his fetish for women's orthopedic shoes. With sweaty palms and a racing pulse he shuffled into the small auditorium at the Centerfield YMCA. Judging by the looks of the characters, misfits and weirdos to either side, the town was home to quite a few with miscellaneous problems.

The group leader wore a nametag that identified him as Philip. He began the meeting with a prayer that didn't exactly reassure Scott that he was on the right path to overcome his fetish: "Lord, you have made some losers, and many of those are here with us today. We all pray for the normalcy you gave to others but denied to us, for reasons you must understand but we don't. You could save us a lot of work, not to mention hours of time, by just fixing what ails us, and that doesn't seem like too much to ask from someone who woke the dead and fed tons of people with a couple of mackerel and some bread. But if that isn't in the grand plan, we'll work here to solve these problems ourselves. Amen."

Philip lifted his head and gazed out over the

audience. "Who is ready to testify?" A hand went up in the back. "Brother Arnold, you are recognized. Tell it."

Brother Arnold, a stoop-shouldered man of fifty, rose to his feet. "My name's Arnold, and I'm a shop-putter."

The crowd responded in unison, "Hi, Arnold."

Philip said, "Now Arnold, you probably need to spend a minute telling us what a shop-puttter is, since I myself have never heard the term, as I suspect others here have never heard it."

"It is the opposite of a shoplifter. I go into places, mostly convenience stores, and while nobody is looking I put things on the shelves. Mostly it is new stuff I buy at other stores, but sometimes I bring used stuff from home. I need help."

Philip asked, "Doesn't it get kinda expensive buying new stuff and then giving it away?"

"That's why I need help. The wife has just about had it with my habits. She said unless I got help she would be putting me someplace, and it wouldn't be a convenience store. I don't guess I can blame her. Sometimes the used stuff I shop-put is hers. Just last week I put her hair dryer in a department store. She was mad as a hornet. When she noticed it was missing, she asked me where I took it, and when I told her she went down there and got it back."

"So it worked out okay," Philip said.

"Not really," said Arnold. "They caught her on a

security camera and arrested her for shoplifting. Her hearing is next week."

"I see," said Philip. "Have you told us everything?"

"It gets worse." Arnold hung his head, seemingly unable to continue.

"Brother Arnold, we're here for you," Philip said, his voice rising. Then, spreading his arms, he said, "Aren't we here for Brother Arnold, Brothers?"

"We're here," shouted the crowd as Scott seriously contemplated a low crawl across the floor to the exit.

"See that, Brother Arnold? We're with you. Tell it all. Get it off your chest. You'll feel so much better."

Arnold managed to raise his head. "Well, I'm not proud of this, but I need to own up. Last week I shop-putted a new blender I bought on sale at Wall-More. Paid $29.95 for it. Nice blender, still in the box. I took it to Park&Pay, that convenience store. I found that little machine that spits out the price tags--you know the ones you can't get off with a blowtorch--and I printed me a label for $429.29 and stuck it over the Wall-More price tag."

"Why did you do that?" Philip wanted to know.

"Why? Cause I'm weird, I guess. I stood at the end of the aisle to watch some guy pick it up. He got that look of horror people get when the prices go so high, and I took joy in his pain. I don't know why. I need help."

The man to Scott's left leaned over to him and

whispered, "What a fucking dope."

Philip said, "Thank you, Brother Arnold, for sharing what we can all agree is a serious problem. Is there another Brother who will testify?"

Scott muttered that it was now or never and rose to his feet. "My name's Scott, and I'm an orthopediphile."

"Uuuhhh," shouted the crowd, followed by cries of "sicko," "scumbag," and "bloodsucker."

"Wait," said Scott, "it's not what you think," but already people were moving away from him.

"You disgust me," spit out Brother Philip. "I hope you rot in the worst section of hell."

Scott tried to explain but the boos and hisses grew so loud that he couldn't be heard. Someone in the back hurled a shoe that hit Scott in the shoulder.

"I think you need to leave," Philip said, and the Brothers roared their agreement.

Scott left and did not look back.

Chapter 18

Ed Learns the Difference Between Fu Yung and Kung Fu

Ed waited in the boarding area of George Bush International to begin his twenty-one-hour flight to China. He patted himself on the back for getting out of his comfort zone by going to a place where the language, culture and attitudes promised to be so profoundly different from those in Centerfield. But he knew the lure of this trip went beyond the exotic, which could be found in equal measure in San Francisco at half the airfare. His prime motivation was the duty he felt to the ultimate consumers of Ed's Barbeque Butter to deliver a fine, flavorful product, and since signing on with Elvis Wu he had become increasingly anxious, fearful of finding Wu's "factory" to be little more than a dilapidated garage filled with contaminated ingredients being dumped into a large, dirty vat stirred by a seven-year-old girl. Then again, Wu had mentioned beautiful Chinese women to attend Ed's every need. Probably more of Wu's sales pitch, Ed reasoned, but suppose it proved true?

Ed's hostess in China was to be Elvis Wu's sister, another source of uncertainty. Ed pictured a short, buck-toothed woman with a flat nose, a weak chin, and skin the color of brown-and-serve biscuits before they were browned or served. But Elvis, as if reading his mind, had insisted otherwise.

"She veddy pretty," Wu had told Ed.

"How old did you say she was?"

"Thirty-five. Never been kissed. I joke."

"And her name is . . ."

"Wing," Wu said.

"Must be some Oriental custom, 'cause no self-respecting American would name a daughter Wing."

Wu laughed. "Not her real name. She not married, so no wing."

Ed's flight began boarding. The first call went out to paraplegics, morons unable to identify their assigned seats without assistance, convicted felons under escort by the U.S. Marshall Service, Plutonium Preferred Members, and children under three traveling alone. Next came the airline's prized membership holders, the Gold Card Suckers, Silver Card Chumps, Bronze Card Also-rans, and Titanium Wanna-Be's. When First Class was announced, Ed stepped forward, only to be scolded for mistakenly lining up in the riff-raff que. He took three steps to the left, thereby uniting with "his people" and avoiding eye contact with the hordes of zones three and four riff-raff waiting to be summoned.

Once aboard, he grew impatient with the large, elderly woman blocking the aisle until he realized it was the flight attendant, a Miss Harris according to her name tag. He ordered two double vodkas and slept until the plane touched down at LAX.

Business Class on China Air was as much like the LAX flight as a 747 resembled the Wright Brothers. A dozen comely, young and lithe women greeted him with smiles that lit up the cabin. The three serving his seating area wore nametags in Chinese with translations below. They were He, Ha, and No, from which Ed concluded that there must be a shortage of letters in the Chinese alphabet, or perhaps for last names the Chinese mandated a one-syllable policy like the one-child policy.

"Hey, He," he called, "I need a drink."

"I am Ha. What would you like"

"Vodka. With a twist."

A minute later the drink was set before him.

"Thanks, Ha," he said.

"I am No."

"I thought you were Ha."

"No."

"No?"

"No."

The combination of several drinks and intense attention from beautiful, doting women put Ed in a frisky mood.

"Say, darlin'," he said to He, or Ha, or No. "What time do you get off work."

"Never," she said.

"Well, this plane has got to land sometime. At least I hope it does. How's about when we get where we're goin', you show me around China. You can't work all the time."

"But we do."

"We work hard in Texas, too, but we leave time to fool around."

"What is 'fool around'?"

"It don't translate too well. I'd have to show you. Maybe hire us one of them little monkeys to pull us around in one of them vegetable carts."

"You mean rickshaw?"

"That's it, rickshaw. So, what say?"

"Must ask my father."

"Good idea. Then I can tell him my intentions are honorable. What does daddy do?"

"He pulls rickshaw."

Ed gulped. "If you're Ha, let's get He over

here."

"No."

Chapter 19

Fran Devotes an Afternoon to Clowning Around

Fran's decision to see Amos Albright came to her one night in the shower. She wasn't consciously thinking about the park, or *The Sentinel,* or much of anything in particular, or so she assumed until this inspiration hit her as she rinsed her hair. Albright owned the most desirable tract of land for a park left in Centerfield. Maybe a visit from her would begin a dialogue leading to success. As she toweled off, she called Kirstin. "Find out anything you can about him, including what else he owns."

Kirstin's effort yielded little beyond what was generally known, almost all of which had come from Flippo Laurens, Albright's distant cousin. She learned his address and a phone number, and with Tricksy's help at the courthouse prepared an inventory of the remarkable amount of land titled in his name. Voting records showed he voted regularly. Fran called him, introduced herself, and asked for an appointment. The response was gruff, monosyllabic, but he agreed. Noting that the address was a few blocks from *The Sentinel's* offices, she walked to the appointment.

Albright's house stood in the middle of a quiet block flanked by houses of similar vintage and construction. A two-story red brick affair, it seemed to reflect its owner, or what Fran anticipated its owner to be like. The shutters needed paint, the landscaping, while neat, was uninspired, and there were several shingles missing from the roof. The house managed to look reclusive. Maybe, thought Fran, the owner needs attention like the house needs attention. She knocked and waited.

Albright opened the door, nodding briefly before saying, "Follow me." He led her through a darkened room that must have been a living room, down a short hallway, and into a room lined with bookshelves on three sides. The fourth side, mostly glass, emitted light. He motioned her to a leather chair she sank into comfortably, while he sat in an identical chair opposite her. "Coffee?" he asked.

"No thank you," she replied, studying him. He must have once been a larger man, but now his skin hung from his frame and had begun to wrinkle with age. This was particularly noticeable in his face, where the sags, creases and gravitational strain produced a profound sadness of expression. Fran thought him on the verge of tears.

"I should probably properly introduce myself," she said, making a conscious effort to smile.

"As you wish," he said, "but I'm well aware of who you are. You edit *The Sentinel*, and you ran for mayor some time back. I voted for you, incidentally."

Fran blushed, which surprised her. With a short laugh she said, "I'm not here soliciting money, so let me put your mind at ease there. I'm sure you get enough of that from others."

"Only by mail," he said. "You're my first visitor in some time. I suppose the locals are afraid of me."

"Why do you think that is?" she asked.

He shrugged. "I live alone, keep to myself, don't go out much. The Boo Radley of Centerfield."

"Aren't you lonely?" Fran asked, not intending to.

"In a word, yes, but it's an old habit now, and I'm an old dog."

"A well-read old dog if these books are any indication."

"Another old habit. I have hundreds of friends between their pages, and none of them give me anything but pleasure. But you didn't come to discuss literature. You came about the park."

Fran glanced down to her hands folded in her

lap. "That's true. It is important to me."

"As everyone who reads *The Sentinel* knows after that editorial you wrote. A fine piece, by the way."

Fran blushed again. She hadn't anticipated any compliments. "So you agree with the need for a park?"

"I do indeed, but if it is my land you have in mind, I doubt the city can afford it."

"You own quite a bit of land here, aside from that tract."

"That's because I began buying it as a young man, before Centerfield was much more than a crossroads and you would have had to pay someone to live here. Land was too cheap to pass up."

"I can't find any record of a sale . . ."

"So, you've done your research. I never sell, a rule I live by."

"Well," said Fran, eying him steadily, "it's none of my business, but what happens to all that property . . ."

"When I die? You're right, it's none of your business, but I don't mind you asking. The truth is I haven't decided. It weighs on my mind more each day. I get calls from developers right and left wanting to buy, and so far I've told them I'm not interested."

"Perhaps," Fran suggested, "the time will come when you want to do something for Centerfield."

"Why should I?"

"Because it's your home, and Centerfield has been good to you, has it not?"

"It is a nice town, as there are many nice towns in this country. I pay my taxes, and in exchange I get basic services. A basic business deal."

"But a town is so much more than a basic business deal. It's spirit, it's people . . ."

"Neither of those interest me much."

"Why did you come here?"

"To be left alone. I never thought it would get this big, this 'progressive'."

Fran was silent for a moment before saying, "There are some very nice design drawings of the park. Very preliminary. Would you mind if I brought them by? I'd like you to see what's being discussed."

"You will have them delivered?"

"No, I thought I'd bring them myself."

Albright nodded. "Any time."

She rose to leave, extending her hand. "It has been a pleasure getting to know you, Mr. Boo Radley. May I call you Boo?" She thought she saw the faintest hint of a smile form on Albright's lips, but she left thinking he was the saddest man she had ever met.

Chapter 20

Let the Recruiting War Begin

When Art learned that an Arab family had moved onto the land Monty now called New P, he fumed silently until Tricksy pressed him to reveal what was on his mind.

"This is a setback for the settlement of New Israel," he said. "Now there will be a flood of Palestinians coming here, and New I has not one resident."

She thought she saw where he was headed. "Art, honey, I just can't live out there. It's too far from work, and I need people around me."

Art shook his head. "I did not mean for us to move. I must find some Jews willing to be settlers. But it is thousands of acres with no improvements and many coyotes. How can I talk anyone into it?"

"So how did that Monty feller get those Arabs to his place?" she asked.

"I heard they came from Detroit. He offered free land."

"So why don't you offer free land? You sure have enough of it out there."

"I do not care for the word 'free'."

"Well I get all that, but think about it, hon. You've got a bizillion acres out there doing nothing. Just because you give away some to get someone out there doesn't mean you have to give away the rest. I think they call it a lost leader or bite and switch."

"Bait and switch," he said. "You may have a point. I will advertise in Houston. There are many good Jews there, and they won't have so far to come."

The next day, Art showed Tricksy the ad he had composed.

> Be the first to claim 100 acres of land absolutely FREE in an exclusive residential community outside Houston. To claim this land, you must be a Jew. Do not think of trying to get this FREE land if you are an Arab, a Christian, a Muslim, a Hindu, a Mormon, a Baptist, or a Rotarian. Jews only. For details, call Art Adams at the number listed below.

"Art, honey, I appreciate what you're trying to do, but that ad is going to get you in trouble. There is this little old law about excluding people based on religion."

"What does this law say?"

"It says you can't do it or you go to jail."

"You mean I can't mention the requirement to be Jewish?"

"I mean you can't exclude others."

"But I don't want any others."

"Well, you're gonna get 'em when they read that ad. You'll have every Methodist in Texas on our doorstep an hour after that is published."

"I will not give the sacred land of New I to a Methodist. Not one acre." Art grew silent before stabbing his finger toward the ceiling in revelation. "I know. I'll run the ad in Hebrew. That way, only a Jew will be able to read it."

"Is that what they speak over there?"

"Mostly Yiddish," he replied.

"That is one good idea," she said. "If only a Jew can read it, you can take out all that language about Mormons so you won't get in trouble and you won't go to jail."

Art's ad ran in the *Houston Chronicle* the following week. He stared at his phone for three days before a caller responded.

"Chaim Levy here," the man said with just a hint of Texas accent. "This business about free land on the level?"

"Not all level," Art answered. "Some rolling

hills."

"I meant, is the ad serious when it says free land?"

"First, I must ask a question. Are you Jewish?"

"With the name Chaim Levy? No, I'm Presbyterian." After a pause, Levy added, "That's a joke."

"In that case," Art said, "I can confirm the offer is real. One hundred acres free."

"How many people live there now?"

"Not many. Fewer than one."

"I see. And are there amenities."

"Yes. Air and water. Okay, not so much water."

"But no roads or sewer."

"The land is flat enough to drive over in most places. You could put in a drain field to handle sewage. These are minor concerns."

"Perhaps for you, but for anyone thinking about living there, they are major. I see now why you are offering free land. And what about the title?"

Art feared this question. After a pause, he said, "I will give you a certificate of ownership. Signed by me. With a seal."

"And I can record that at the courthouse?"

Tricksy worked in the record room of the courthouse, but whether a mere certificate, purchased from a novelty shop in town, could be recorded Art didn't know.

"I'll have to get back to you on that one," he told Chaim.

Chapter 21

Kirstin takes on Mayor Buster

Fran asked Kirstin to cover Mayor Bustamonte's ribbon cutting at The Dancing Doughnut, a fast-growing chain opening its first store in Centerfield.

"Just what we need," said Kirstin with a sigh. "Another doughnut shop. I bet every diabetic in town will be there."

Fran said, "They must have found a niche. Find out what makes a dancing doughnut special."

Kirstin arrived early and had little trouble persuading the manager, Dancing Glenn according to his name tag, to give her a tour.

"We're making a fresh batch for the ceremony," he said. "Would you like to watch?"

"Love it," said Kirstin.

He led her back to the kitchen, to a large copper kettle, by which stood a fresh-face young girl wearing the Dancing Doughnut uniform.

"This is Dancing Judy," said Dancing Glenn. "She's about to demonstrate what makes our doughnuts so special. Dancing Judy, this is Kirstin from *The Sentinel*. She's going to write a story on us, so we want to bring her our A game."

Dancing Judy bounced on the balls of her feet with excitement.

"Oh," she said breathlessly, "these doughnuts are soooo good." She placed her hand lightly on the rim of the kettle. "In here we have the Dancing Doughnut dough, made with a secret formula that only our founder knows. It would be good enough by itself, but then we add that special touch that makes us unique." Dancing Judy's pride in her employer was reflected by the beam of her smile. "I'll do that now." She reached up and pulled a lever.

Kirstin heard a rumble as the chute opened and hundreds of small, pebble-like objects descended into the kettle. "Those look like peanut M&Ms," she said.

"They ARE peanut M&Ms," said Dancing Judy, bouncing again. After two minutes, the rumble ceased and the chute closed. "It's programmed," she explained. "Once it reaches ten thousand, it shuts off."

She then pressed a button which lowered into the kettle a stainless-steel beater that had been hidden from Kirstin's view by a metal partition. The beater began to turn. "When everything is all mixed in, the mixture goes here," she said, pointing to a metal pipe. "That leads to the forms, where the dough is molded into our signature shape."

Kirstin played a hunch. "Let me guess. Your doughnuts have no holes."

Dancing Judy laughed. "Silly. You can't have a doughnut without a hole. It's illegal. I read that somewhere. No, our doughnuts have holes, but they are shaped like this." She held up a mold for Kirstin's inspection.

"That looks like a Bundt cake mold."

"I thought the same thing. It's actually smaller, so our Dancing Doughnuts weigh a uniform one and a half pounds."

"Each?" said Kirstin, unable to hide her shock.

"Each."

"So a dozen weighs . . . eighteen pounds?"

"Precisely," said Dancing Judy, bouncing again. "The M&Ms melt in the dough, giving us the most delicious doughnut in America."

"Thank you so much for the tour, Dancing Judy. I think I hear the mayor beginning his speech, so I need to run."

Outside, Mayor Bustamonte stood behind a small dais emblazoned with the Centerfield seal. The seal had only recently been designed by Rosalinda

Bustamonte, the mayor's sister, and featured in its center crossed baseball bats and a ball, above which hovered the silhouette of a man bearing close resemblance in profile to the mayor.

Kirstin took her place in a folding chair facing the dais. Many seated around her she knew to be Bustamontes.

Mayor Buster began by thanking all the city employees who had worked so hard to pass the zoning variance, issued the building permit, performed the inspections, licensed the business, and come to the ceremony. After some additional thank-yous, he got down to business.

"When the representatives of The Dancing Doughnut came to tell me they were considering a franchise here in Centerfield, I asked them, 'Will it employ our local workers to build the building?' They said yes, and employing workers is a good thing. Then I asked our city treasurer, Ronaldo Bustamonte, to estimate the sales and real estate taxes The Dancing Doughnut will generate, and they are significant, which is another good thing. Then I learned that this business will employ twelve people, from managers to janitors, and that is a good thing. When I was elected, I promised 'good things, si, bad things, no,' so I am keeping my pledge to the people of our city and I say 'Welcome, Dancing Doughnut."

Kirstin raised her hand. "Mr. Mayor, according to my research, each Dancing Doughnut contains 3500 calories. At a time when the city and the country are experiencing an obesity epidemic, is it possible that such a product, which after all has zero nutritional value, is a bad thing?"

Buster did not immediately answer, appearing to ponder the question. Finally, he said, "Yes, many calories with no nutrition is a bad thing."

"So," she followed up, "how do you reconcile a bad thing with your pledge to do good things?"

Buster began to look visibly uncomfortable, blinking excessively and shifting his weight from foot to foot. Then he broke into a smile. "But I listed three good things, and you named only one bad thing, so The Dancing Doughnut is a good thing, yes?"

Kirstin pressed. "Suppose I listed the health care costs of treating the obese, and the lost productivity of people who can't control their weight, and the shorter life spans of the morbidly obese."

"Yes, those are all bad things."

"Four bad things, by my count. So does that make The Dancing Doughnut a bad thing?"

An aide rushed to the dais and whispered into Buster's ear. He nodded several times, glancing toward Kirstin. Then he said, "No, because we have two weight loss clinics in Centerfield, and those businesses will benefit from people who need to lose weight. So that makes five good things to four bad things, so The Dancing Doughnut is a good thing." Buster gave his signature swoosh and left the dais before Kirstin could ask another question.

Chapter 22

*The Abdullahs adapt
to life in New P*

The Abdullah family had seen life turned on its head since leaving Detroit for Texas, and although life was not perfect, they had never been happier. Halim framed the deed, which Monty had purchased from the same novelty store from which Art purchased his certificate for land in New I. Like Art, Monty signed the certificate. Halim hung it over the door of the double-wide so that each of them would see it when leaving, a constant reminder that they <u>owned</u> the land on which they were about to set foot. The Abdullah family, formerly of Detroit and very formerly of Palestine, owned an acre of land in Texas, U.S.A. A dream come true, and nothing less.

As to "not perfect," there were adjustments to be made. Hessa found work at once, the Golden Glop having lost a waitress and constantly short-staffed. Lindsey, the cynical waitress who had served George and Joyce, trained Hessa, warning her in their first session together that, no matter how hungry Hessa might get, she should not to eat the food. Hessa heeded the advice.

The adjustment for Halim proved slightly greater, as exactly one driver-owned taxi patrolled Centerville's streets and there was no demand for another. But Halim, before driving a Detroit hack, had spent several years as an auto mechanic, and the demand for those exceeded supply thanks to the persistent recession that induced residents to fix up old clunkers rather than risk cardiac arrest by perusing showroom sticker prices. Big Al hired Halim and taught him to drive the wrecker. Hessa and Halim drove the old van into town every day. He dropped her at the Golden Glop, returning at her shift change to pick her up.

Monty knew that the key to long term happiness for the Abdullahs would be provisions for the children. He interviewed dozens of candidates for a tutor. Many objected to the long drive, fifty miles round trip across barren land. Several expressed reservations about teaching "the foreign element," as one beehive hairdo had put it. At last, he found a person who fit the most critical qualifications: reliable, great references, academically proficient, eager to teach. One small red flag surfaced when Arlene Simpson displayed a large cross around her neck during the interview, but this was Texas, after all, and Monty assumed that those candidates who didn't wear crosses to the interview had them in the top drawer at home. Arlene got the job.

For several weeks this arrangement pleased everyone. Najair and Rayya liked Arlene, who enjoyed them, and Hessa and Halim brought home good money from their respective employers. Every evening after dinner, the Abdullahs walked their land, reveling in its vastness when compared to the 1200 square foot apartment in Detroit that had been the outer limits of their prior world. On weekends, they fixed a picnic and sat beneath the mesquite tree at the edge of the property. The doublewide loomed in the distance, but as far as they were concerned they had escaped to Shangri La. On one such picnic, Hessa had just served her special tuna fish sandwiches when Rayya began singing softly, more or less to herself.

"Rayya, what are you singing?" asked her father.

"Jesus loves me."

Hessa and Halim exchanged looks.

"Do you know any other songs?" Hessa asked.

"Yes," said the girl with a hint of pride. "I know 'What a friend we have in Jesus'."

"Did Miss Arlene teach you those?"

Rayya nodded.

Halim shrugged. "I guess we should have expected that in Texas. At least it's not Hava Nagila.

Chapter 23

Fran eyes Olivia as
Olivia Woos Roger

Back at the pit, Roger organized his students into teams and shifts. Fran accustomed herself to the new rhythms of plinking hammers and the occasional cry of discovery. Because activities in the pit were invisible to her from the house, she fell into the habit of standing at the rim, observing.

One woman in the pit drew Fran's focus, as the woman seemed more interested in Roger than in archaeology. Fran judged her to be about twenty-five, very perky, with frequent questions that required visits to wherever Roger happened to be working. On a couple of visits, Fran saw her squeeze Roger's hand, from which she concluded they were an item. Olivia, as Fran learned her name to be, had some rather obvious charms, extremely good tennis-anyone looks and well proportioned, as revealed by high-cut shorts and braless tank tops.

Late one afternoon, Fran happened to look out her kitchen window as the crew wrapped up digging operations for the day. Roger and Olivia, alone at the van, lingered in a dry, dusty embrace that Fran found sensuous despite the absence of a romantic setting. It filled her with profound longing. Beyond an occasional trashy novel full of steam and lust, she rarely dwelt on physical intimacy. But watching Roger and Olivia, their hands intertwined, her head on his chest, her tiptoeing to whisper something into his ear, reminded her that her window for finding a life partner was closing. In a few years she would confront menopause, and then the empty nest. Did she want a life partner? She knew that Jim was irreplaceable, but did that mean the perfect was the enemy of the good? Most people, she suspected, went through life without ever meeting the perfect match. Because she had married one, and she was statistically unlikely to meet another, should she settle for forty or fifty years of solitude, made worse on the day Sarah left for college? Something in the lingering embrace outside her window made her wonder, for the first time, if she had <u>really</u> dealt with Jim's loss, and now that she was approaching forty-one, it was high time she did so. But how?

Days later, Fran came home from a particularly grueling day at *The Sentinel*. She fixed dinner, read with Sarah, and when the house was quiet treated herself to a glass of wine. She had taken her first satisfying sip when she heard a knock at the door. She opened it to find Roger. So used was she to seeing him covered with dust that it took her a moment to recognize him.

"I showered before I came over," he said, as if reading her mind. "Do you have a minute?"

"Of course. Come in."

Roger walked in, a faint aroma of aftershave trailing as he passed.

"Glass of wine?" Fran asked. "Any kind you want as long as it's chardonnay."

"Love it," said Roger. He accepted the proffered glass and leaned against the counter. "What's up?" he asked.

"Well, let's see," said Fran. "Putin has put Russia firmly under his thumb, North Korea is again acting like the lunatic state it always has been, China is stealing our jobs and manipulating its currency, Japan is still in shock from the tsunami, Italy, Greece, Spain and Portugal are about to dive into the tank, Germany is behaving German-like, Mexico is where Columbia was twenty years ago, Canada looks better by the day, Texas is threatening to secede, again, and here in dear old Centerfield the fate of a much needed park rests on the whim of a clown-- literally. Oh, and the Arab spring has turned to winter and the Israelis and Palestinians still haven't figured out how to get along. Glad you asked?"

"You didn't mention the giant hole at the end of your driveway."

"I was hoping you could cover that one, no pun intended."

"We sent some finds off last week. Depending on what the lab comes back with, we may not be here as long as you think."

"Let's not talk about the pit," she said. "One of your students seems particularly enthused, and not over archaeology."

Roger grinned. "Olivia's okay. She has some growing up to do, as I've told her."

"You been together long, not that it's any of my business?"

"We dated a few times before this dig started. I have a rule against dating my students, but somehow she wrangled her way into this project."

"She sounds resourceful."

"More like aggressive."

Fran sipped her wine and studied him. His eyes were bluer in the fluorescent light overhead. "You're looking for shy and retiring? Again, not that it is any of my business."

"I'm not looking for anything except a ring-tailed scorpion. If something comes along . . ."

"I wish you had been here a few months ago. A woman who works for me, Kirstin, might have been a fit. Now she's in love."

Roger nodded before saying, "I really like Scott. I talk to him while he's out there washing cars. Great kid."

"Thank you. Praise for my children never gets old."

"And your daughter . . ."

"Sarah."

"Sarah is going to break some hearts, but I suppose you know that."

"Yes, but the breaks go both ways. You can have yours broken, and that hurts."

"Speaking from experience?" He paused and grinned. "Not that it's any of my business."

"Maybe not the kind you think. My husband Jim was killed in a traffic accident a few years back. Another glass of wine?"

"Make it a half. I'm driving."

"You haven't told me why you're here."

"Just passing by and wanted to thank you for being so patient with all this. Plus all the lemonade."

"You're welcome. You didn't need to make a special trip, but I appreciate it. Any idea of how much longer the pit will be a pit?"

"It all depends on the lab reports we should be getting next week. If the samples prove we're in a pre-Clovis mine, I may retire here."

Chapter 24

George Eyes the Prize

George stepped onto the scales, both happy and sad at the digital readout of 348 pounds; happy because it meant his splurge had another twelve pounds to run, and sad because he felt certain he had been packing it on at a more competitive pace. It was the stress brought on by these crazy grave robbers. Stress, he knew, was a calorie burner. More starches, he told himself.

Following his physical, George lost no time in filling his prescription for Testosterall, the latest ED drug, widely advertised by a virile couple sitting in a bathtub--the same bathtub--escalated to the top of a roller coaster. The tub paused briefly at the apex, time to allow a knowing kiss before plunging downward. As the tub descended, the man's right arm shot up in phallic triumph, while the woman draped one arm languidly over the side in a gesture that had been the subject of a number of interpretations. This ad ran three hundred times a day on the minor networks, there no longer being any major networks. The voiceover, obviously written by the Testosterall legal department, disclaimed: Take only as prescribed. Risks include instant death, hideous disfigurement you-know-where, hives, upset stomach, and a delayed tax refund. For erections lasting longer than eight hours, seek emergency help.

As he left the prescription counter, George shook the vial of green tablets like dice in Vegas. This was not inappropriate, as to exercise conjugal privileges he would need to get very lucky. Joyce kept to a strict, well-worn routine where sex was concerned--twice a year except in Maine, and this wasn't his month.

But just when he was beginning to despair, he did get lucky. Joyce came bounding into the den in a paroxysm of excitement.

"George, you'll never guess," she said, on the verge of hyperventilation.

George hit the mute button on the remote control. "I can't guess."

"Try."

"Give me a hint."

Joyce flapped her hands like a duck seeking liftoff from a pond. "Okay, a hint. Shawn Pen and Centerfield."

"Then I'm going to guess that Shawn Pen is

coming to Centerfield."

"Yes!" she exclaimed, and with such passion that he was reminded of the Testosterall tablets. This has possibilities, he thought.

Joyce continued. "I just got an email from SPHINCTER, announcing his visit next spring. Do you think we can throw a party for him?"

"How long is he staying?"

"They didn't say. It probably depends on his movie schedule and whether there is a humanitarian crisis somewhere. Oh, this is too exciting."

Her euphoria carried over into the evening, so after a glass of wine George brought up the subject of his own humanitarian crisis and suggested they retire early to the bedroom. Joyce hesitated.

"George, are you sure? Things haven't been working so well for you down there."

"You had your surprise today and now I have one for you. Dr. Malloy gave me a prescription for Testosterall."

"Those people in the bathtub?"

"The same."

"You have some?"

"I do."

"Does it work?"

"I haven't tried it, but there's no time like the

present."

"In that case I'll slip away and put on my bunny pajamas. You always liked those."

"Great idea. That will give me time to pop a pill. The directions say to allow thirty minutes."

George took a pill. Ten minutes later Joyce beckoned him to the bedroom with a sultry, "G-e-o-r-g-i-e." He found her in bed in the bunny pjs. She wiggled the cotton tail flirtatiously. He undressed and climbed into bed.

She unbuttoned the first three buttons and parted the fur enough to expose most of her breast. "Anything happening?"

"Nothing. Guess I need more time."

"We could watch TV," she said.

"How about a hand of strip poker. It will get us in the mood."

"Will you show me how to play?"

Of course." He went to his bureau and took a deck of cards from the top drawer. He shuffled them, then fanned them out, face down. "Pick a card," he told her.

She drew one.

"What is it?" he asked.

"The four of Clubs."

"You lose. Take off your pajamas."

"Are you sure that's how it's played? Besides, it doesn't appear to me that anything is happening you-know-where."

"Yeah, and it's been half an hour. Maybe I should take another."

"Are you sure?"

"Why not? I'm a big guy. I probably need double the dose that wimps take."

"Maybe we should consult Dr. Malloy."

"Like he's going to be available at this time of night."

"Well, your little bunny can wait until another night to go hopping down the bunny trail."

"Yeah, I know, Easter's on its way. But I can't wait until Easter. I'm taking another pill."

Two minutes later he emerged from the bathroom. "The directions say Testosterall tablets are blue."

"So?"

"So the ones they gave me at the pharmacy are green."

"Then what did you take?"

"Beats me. I guess I'll find out."

Chapter 25

Chaim Makes an Impulse Buy

Chaim Levy drove to Centerfield with no serious intention of moving there. But as a student of the Zionist movement, he found himself captivated by the notion that some Israeli named Art was engaged in engineering Zion 2.0.

Art meet Chaim at the gas station just outside Centerfield. A firm handshake and solid eye contact impressed Art as belonging to someone he could do business with. In Art's pickup, they drove until they reached a cluster of cacti just off the edge of the highway.

"New I starts here," Art said, a touch of pride evident in his voice.

"I gotta give it to you, Art. This is a bold plan. Bold with a capital B."

The pickup left the highway and for the next several hours Art pointed out New I's most dramatic features: dry creek beds; gently rolling flatland leading to not-so-gently rolling land; a spot Art called "Lookout Point" that was precisely nine feet above sea level; a boulder formation that looked to

Art like a squirrel sitting on its hind legs if he squinted and applied some imagination; a tree hit by lightning recently, judging by the fresh wood at the fissure. Art seized every opportunity to emphasize the vastness of the property while Chaim nodded at the appropriate points, said little, and asked few questions until Art began explaining how he had managed to acquire options on all the property they were traversing. Back at the cacti cluster, Art turned off the engine and looked meaningfully at Chaim, who knew what Art wanted to hear.

"Let's be honest, Art," Chaim said. "What you have here is a noble idea and miles of dirt."

"And our fathers and their fathers thought the land of Israel was just miles of desert. They were right, of course, but look at it now."

"Beautiful, to be sure, but look where you and I live."

"Too many problems," they said simultaneously.

"So Chaim, what would it take to get you to become the first resident of New I?"

Chaim's face contorted into a frown. "On the phone you mentioned one hundred acres."

"FREE acres of your choice."

"And some kind of certificate. Signed by you."

"Yes."

"Not good enough."

"I'll throw in an espresso maker."

"Okay, here are my terms. One thousand acres of land, my choice, and an option to purchase those acres for $1.00 if and when New I exercises its options to buy all this property."

"You want to buy an option on an option?"

"For $1.00. And I'll take the certificate. What a souvenir that will make."

Art rubbed his chin. "You drive a hard bargain."

Chaim extended his hand. "Do we have a deal?"

Art hesitated, but not for long. He shook Chaim's hand. "You have a deal." Then, after a pause, he added, "On one condition."

Chaim's eyebrows shot up. "Condition? What condition? We shook hands."

"That you build a house on your land, starting not later than sixty days from today. And that you move into the house when finished."

"And what if New I never exercises its options? My house will sit on land I don't own."

"A technical flaw, I admit."

"So how about this? If New I doesn't close on its options, you buy the house from me."

Art took a deep breath. "If New I doesn't close, I may have to come live with you. Everything I have is tied up in the commissions I've earned but won't be paid until the deal is done."

Chaim was silent for a moment, canting his head to one side as he stared at the horizon. "Tell you what. In Jerusalem, they are still fighting over ownership of the temple. Two thousand years they've been arguing. Maybe title anxiety is part of being a Jew. You have a deal."

Art hit the steering wheel in triumph. "Wonderful! Now we should pick out your land."

"I know the place," said Chaim. "Remember the rocks you said looked like a squirrel?"

"Yeah."

"I saw a beaver. But that's my land."

Chapter 26

West Meets East,
Ed Meets Wing

Ed stepped off the plane in China in something of an alcoholic fog, so it took him a long moment to register the sign, printed in English, for "Mr. Ed," but not even the fatigue he felt and the vodka he had consumed could obscure what he noticed at once: the woman holding the sign, Elvis Wu's sister Wing, was one pretty lady. Tall for a Chinese, she had a shapely face, tapered legs and a broad smile. Ed's mood improved, his rejection by He, or Ha, or No already a distant memory.

Wing bowed faintly at the waist as Ed approached. "Welcome to China, Mr. Ed."

Ed wasn't certain of the protocol; should he bow? Extend his hand? He also wasn't certain where he was. The itinerary listed a destination with an unpronounceable name beginning with G, so Ed had told the boys at the club he was landing in the G spot. He hadn't bothered to locate it on a map. Wing lowered her sign and stared at him, for precisely what he was equally uncertain. He wished Fran was here to put things right. He sensed that throwing a big old Texas arm around Wing accompanied by "Howdy, Darlin'" was not the perfect response. High five? Fist pump? He settled on a question: "Where are we, anyway?"

Wing smiled. He noticed her dimples, unaware that Chinese women had dimples.

"You in Guangzhou. Americans know it by former name, Canton."

"Oh," said Ed. "Football Hall of Fame is in Canton."

"My brother says I must make you welcome. Supply every need."

"That brother of yours is a piece of work."

"Piece of work?"

"A little expression back home that means he's one of a kind. So thoughtful of him to think about my every need."

Ed felt the fog of the flight lifting as he mentally drew up a list of his every need to be satisfied by the beautiful woman who greeted him.

"What's our plan, Wing? May I call you Wing?"

She nodded. "You are tired from your long trip. Perhaps a hot bath at the hotel?"

"I don't suppose that tub is big enough for two."

"Big enough for six."

She gave his claim checks to a skycap and led him to a limousine waiting at the curb. He could see the city in the distance, thinking one building might hold the entire population of Centerfield. By the time they reached his hotel he had a new perspective on China. Wing and the limo returned that evening to take him to dinner. She ordered for him without looking at the menu.

"Say, what is this stuff?" he asked, diving into a soup-like substance in a ceramic bowl.

"Better not to ask," she said. "You like it?"

"You bet."

On the day scheduled for the factory tour, Ed and Wing started early. When their driver pulled up to the plant, Ed emitted a low whistle. "I thought we did things big in Texas," he said. "That's the biggest building I've ever seen."

"Five thousand workers," Wing said, the pride she took in impressing the American written on her face. "Three shifts. Makes lots of things."

"Yeah, like Ed's Barbeque Butter that doesn't taste like motor oil." He winked at her to make sure she knew he was teasing. Wing was beginning to grow on him.

They entered a small reception area furnished

only with four plastic chairs, a basic wooden coffee table with Chinese magazines spread across it, and an empty umbrella stand.

"Wait here," Wing instructed. "I need to find out the station number." She walked to a secure door, punched in a code, placed her hand palm down on a reader, and waited. A green light over the door flashed on as the door slid open. She slipped inside. Before the door closed, Ed caught a glimpse of a cavernous factory. Minutes later, Wing emerged. "Ready to walk?"

A door Ed had not noticed slid open. On the other side they were met by two young women, who helped them into white scrubs, sanitary head covers, and booties that fit over their shoes. As he was being prepped, Ed gazed around. "I do believe you could fit about four Texas Stadiums in here."

"What is Texas Stadium?"

"A pretty big place where I come from. For football."

They walked for what seemed to Ed like miles. White-clad workers on either side of them took no notice, intent on the tasks at hand. Men and women on Segways zipped around them, but they too appeared to take no notice of the visitors. At last Wing stopped at a station where the numbers 1026 were printed in Chinese, English and French. In it four workers, all women, operated a vat-like crucible not unlike the one at the Dancing Doughnut.

"They mixing your sauce," Wing told him. "I see if any ready yet."

She spoke rapid Chinese to a woman who wore a red head cover. The others wore blue. "A supervisor," Wing explained. "Batch made this morning is ready for inspection."

The supervisor brought a small tray, on which rested two paper cups, each with a small spoon. Ed took one, handed it to Wing, then picked up the other. He positioned his nose over it as if a sommelier had just served him a vintage merlot.

"Doesn't smell like motor oil," he said, winking again. He lifted the spoon to his mouth, took a small taste, then looked toward the ceiling to appraise what he savored. "Something is missing."

Wing tasted hers. "Delicious," she pronounced.

"Delicious, yes, but what's missing?"

Wing returned to the supervisor, who extracted a paper encased in plastic from a folder, the ingredient list. Wing translated as Ed nodded with each ingredient read. The last ingredient was fig extract.

"No," said Ed. "Not fig. I specified prune juice.

That's what's missing."

Wing looked crestfallen. "I am very sorry, Mr. Ed. Prunes no good here. Figs very good."

"No doubt, but that guy on the label gave me the secret recipe and it calls for prune juice. A prune is a prune and a fig is a fig." He paused, looking into the distance. "I guess this isn't going to work after all. I'll have to call your brother to tell him I'm going to get a U.S. supplier."

"I understand," said Wing. "Elvis will be sad. He does not like to lose a customer."

Back in the car, Ed said, "Well, now that we've got the business out of the way, how's about you and me spending some quality time under the covers and between the sheets."

Wing said, "Okay."

Ed couldn't hide his surprise. "Okay, as in yes?"

"Yes."

"And you understand what I mean by under the covers and between the sheets?"

"You want to put American hotdog in Chinese bun."

"Yep, I guess you do understand. Well, let's get back to the hotel and get the party started."

"We get married now?"

"Married?"

She nodded. "Must have wing or no bun."

Ed frowned. "We don't usually do it that way in Texas."

"You in China."

"The thing is, you and I have spent time together and I really like you."

"I like you, too, Mr. Ed."

"Have you ever been to Texas?"

"I visit Elvis once in Virginia."

"Virginia's nice, but there's no place like Texas. Is your passport current?"

She nodded.

"Then I guess I need to reserve you a seat. How soon can you leave?"

"Now," she said.

"My kind of woman."

Chapter 27

Wing meets Fran

Ed and Wing landed in Houston after an all-night flight from China. He drove straight to the offices of *The Sentinel,* not so much to catch up on what had happened in his absence as to gauge Fran's reaction to Wing. On the flight he had described her as his "right hand lady," a phrase that took some explaining. Wing had assumed they were lovers. Ed denied that while admitting it wasn't for lack of effort on his part. Wing expressed reluctance to meet such an important person in Ed's life after a twenty-three-hour flight, but he assured her she looked as fresh as if she "just stepped out of a Texas spring shower," which he intended as a compliment.

"I don't know what I did before Fran came and I sure don't know what we would do without her now," he had said. "We were a struggling weekly until she came along, and soon we'll be a daily."

"Is that wise?" asked Wing. "Newspapers have hard time now. Many closings."

"Yeah, there is that, but Fran will figure it out. I just need to stay out of her way."

"How you do that?"

"Golf, mostly. You ever play golf?"

"No, but I quick learner."

"Good. We'll play us some golf."

Fran came out of her office to greet them.

Ed said, "Fran, I'd like you to meet Wing. She showed me around China so I thought I'd return the favor and show her around Texas."

Fran extended her hand. "Nice to meet you, Wing."

Wing grasped her hand, bowed slightly at the waist, then said, "Wing not real name."

Ed registered surprise. He had called her Wing so long he had forgotten she had an unpronounceable Chinese name.

Wing said, "Mr. Ed say you number one employee."

Fran cut her eyes at Ed as something close to a smirk formed on her lips. "Mr. Ed, is it? I like that name."

Ed cleared his throat. "That will be entirely enough of that."

Fran said, "So Wing—may I call you Wing— how long will you be staying in Centerfield?

Wing looked at Ed, who said, "Possibly forever."

Fran's eyebrows arched. "Mr. Ed, this is quite a surprise."

He avoided her stare. "Yeah, I'm a little surprised myself."

"I not surprised," said Wing, winking at Fran.

"Wing took me on a tour of the plant where her brother was making my butter. An amazing operation, but I think I need to move the manufacturing back here where I can keep an eye on it. Any news here? Have they recruited you to run for the U.S. Senate yet?"

"No," said Fran, "but there is talk of the next mayoral race."

"You should have won last time. Next time we'll make it happen."

Chapter 28

Joyce has IDrone issues

Because she used her IDrone daily to access the
SPHINCTER application, Joyce could boast of
reasonable proficiency where her favorite charity was
concerned, and she did. For other applications she
was less successful. George suggested she take a
class, an idea she rejected because she was, she said,
a "hands-on learner through trial and error." Some of
those errors proved mere irritations. Case in point,
the ice maker app. When fumbling for the phone in
her purse, she invariably turned it off. This
aggravated George, who returned from work after a
day dealing with death, parking his car near the pit,
navigating his way through the mesquite trees, all in
anticipation of his vodka martinis, only to find
standing water where the ice cubes should have been.
He snapped at Joyce, who assured him it was an
innocent mistake that could have happened to
anyone.

Because it was free, she also downloaded a
washer-dryer app, a program hyped to save water by
allowing the user to start wash cycles in the middle of

the night. Exactly how that saved any water was not explained, but Joyce loved the idea that while she slept a necessary but routine household chore like laundry could be initiated. But in the initial setup, she somehow programed it to start the washer at 4 a.m. on a daily basis. After a week, during which the washer dutifully began its cycles at the appointed time, she realized that she was wasting vast amounts of water because she failed to load the washer before going to bed. She searched for the setting which would allow her to turn off the "daily" switch, but she could not find it.

But the application that proved most problematic was the one that started her car on command from anywhere in the world. On first view, the car starter application, "Sparky," seemed highly useful. The Texas heat was brutal in an enclosed area like the garage, where during summer months the inside temperature reached the mid-90s. With the tap of a Sparky icon, the app allowed her to start the car and thereby cool it. Joyce, dressed for a day of shopping in her expensive outfits, could step from the air-conditioned house, endure a few steps of blistering heat, and then slide into the bracing comfort of a car perfectly cooled to 68 degrees. The first time she used it, tapping the icon fifteen minutes before her departure, she bubbled over with satisfaction, swearing that the $149 she spent for the app was the best investment she could make. But the icon proved quite sensitive, so that the slightest pressure activated it. The first time this happened actually proved a benefit. Joyce was shopping in a department store. While reaching for a credit card with which to pay for a modest $600 dress she had to have, her knuckle brushed the icon. Minutes later, in the parking lot, she found the car running and cooled. Terrific, she thought, realizing that she could activate it coming and going.

Sparky's next performance should have been its last. Just before going to bed, Joyce placed her IDrone on the night stand in such a manner as to activate the icon, although the following day she swore that was impossible. The car started and ran all night, which would have cost the Fafalones only half a tank of gas had not the family cat, coincidentally also named Sparky, been trapped in the garage. When George entered the garage the next morning, Joyce's car still purred but Sparky did not.

He returned to the house. "Congratulations, Joyce, you asphyxiated the cat. That application has got to go."

Traumatized by the mistake, Joyce tried to

uninstall the Sparky application, but through her tears over the loss of Sparky the cat she was unable to do so.

Chapter 29

The Cold War Turns Hot

Chaim's selection of his one thousand acres was both fortunate and "not-so-much." The boulder formation that for Art looked like a squirrel and to Chaim resembled a beaver gave Beaver Ranch a distinctive landmark and a grand view, but had they driven the perimeter of the sprawling acreage, they might have noticed Halim's doublewide in the distance, for by coincidence, blind luck, fate, karma, whatever, Chaim's chosen land lay just across the arroyo from the Abdullah family.

Good to his word, Chaim broke ground on his house within the sixty days promised to Art. The route for suppliers and workers took them nowhere near the arroyo. Six months later, Chaim's five thousand square foot house, his hacienda, was complete. He threw a massive housewarming, well attended by friends and members of his temple back in Houston, most of whom, between bites of smoked lox, whispered how tragic it was that Chaim had, in the words of Mitzi Birnbaum, "lost his goddamn mind."

Naturally, Art was there, glad-handing guests, speaking some Yiddish, and subtly trolling for more New I residents with off-hand comments like "I'll make you a very good deal." The terms of the deal Chaim had received were not disclosed, Art having sworn Chaim to secrecy as part of that agreement. Art gave out some business cards and thought he detected some mild interest from several guests.

In the weeks following the party, Art made periodic trips to Chaim at Beaver Ranch. With only one resident in New I, it was essential to keep that resident happy. And at least once a week they lunched together in town. In one such lunch, Art discussed the ongoing negotiations with Fran, in which Chaim took limited interest, nodding absently until the conversation turned to OYVEY's options, for it was the exercise of those options that would allow Chaim to secure his title.

"But the two are related," Art insisted over tuna fish. "The negotiations with Fran are all about Monty agreeing to sell. And now, since those Detroit people got a deed for ten acres, we have to deal with them, too."

"Detroit people?"

"Yeah. Arabs, I guess. I hear the guy is a pretty good mechanic."

Chaim said, "Just as long as they know their place. You can't trust them."

"I doubt you'll have any trouble with them. You're probably twenty or thirty miles from them at least."

"Oh? Where do they live?"

"Beats me," Art said. It was a new phrase he had mastered in his effort to pick up American colloquialisms.

A few days later, on one of Art's visits to Beaver Ranch, Chaim suggested they drive the perimeter. "You know," said Chaim, "I've never even laid eyes on parts of what I own."

Art decided it was best not to remind him that, technically, he didn't own anything yet. "Great, let's travel," Art said, employing another colloquialism.

It was about dark when they drove the last section, the part of Chaim's land that bordered the arroyo.

"What's that?" Chaim said, pointing ahead.

"What?"

"Up there. It looked like a small meteor."

"I didn't see anything," Art said.

"Look, there it is again."

This time Art saw it. "Shooting star?"

"That close to earth? No way. And whatever it

is just landed."

Chaim sped up. When they reached the point where the object appeared to land, they got out of the truck and walked into the cone of light provided by the headlights. Chaim bent down and picked up a long stick, charred at one end. "I knew it," he said, raising the stick for Art's inspection. "A rocket."

Art said, "I think they call them bottle rockets."

"A rocket is a rocket," Chaim said. He picked up three more nearby.

They turned and gazed across the arroyo, the direction from which the flash had come. The lights of the Abdullahs' doublewide shown in the distance.

"That must be the Arabs," yelled Chaim. "I'm under attack."

Art shook his head, dazed. He had never seen Chaim so animated. "It . . . can't be. What are the odds?"

"I don't know about odds, but I can't have Arabs shooting rockets onto my land."

"No, of course not," Art mumbled. "I'll get on it right away."

At home later that night, Art related to Tricksy what had happened.

"Bottle rockets?" she said. "Well, who gives a flying fuck about those little old things? I was shooting them off at five. We aimed them at the dog. Inside the house. My momma warned us someone was going to get blinded but no one ever did. Parents just make up things to scare kids. Like momma telling me that if I kept having sex at thirteen something bad was going to happen. She was right about that one."

"Did he offer to marry you?"

"Who?"

"The man who caused the bad thing to happen."

"Oh, I never knew which one it was. Five boyfriends is a lot to keep track of when you're thirteen. But I think your buddy Chaim needs to lighten up."

Chapter 30

World Peace Takes a Hit

Fran now referred to the Art-Monty negotiations as "the quest for world peace." Laughing as she said it, she realized humor would be essential if she was to continue. At the next session (Conference Room, B), she needed all the patience she could muster.

Art cleared his throat and asked to speak first.

"Of course," Fran said.

"I regret to tell you," he began, "that there has been an act of terrorism directed against the state of New Israel. A violation of sovereignty. A dangerous precedent." Even Art knew this was laying it on a bit thick, but Chaim's reaction had shaken him, and he couldn't afford the displeasure of New I's sole resident.

Fran placed both palms on the table. "For the record, Art, there is no sovereign state of New Israel, this being the very sovereign state of Texas. What is the act of terrorism?"

"Rockets were fired onto the property of my resident, Chaim Levy. I was there at the time and witnessed the attack."

Monty scoffed audibly. "Blaming us, I suppose, as usual."

Art responded. "The only house within ten miles of the attack belongs to your settlers, the Abdullahs. Of course I blame them."

"Hold on," said Fran. "What kind of rockets?"

"Small rockets. Limited damage, <u>this</u> <u>time</u>."

"How small?" asked Fran.

"Very small."

"As long as this conference room?"

"Smaller," admitted Art with a hint of sheepishness.

Fran extended her arms. "Longer than this?"

"Not quite," said Art. He held his hands a foot apart. "About like this."

"And the damage?"

"Scars on the ground. Plus, it frightened Chaim and me. Emotional distress."

Monty rolled his eyes. "Next you'll be asking for reparations."

"Not this time. In the interests of peace we are willing to turn a blind cheek."

Fran said, "I think you mean turn the other cheek."

"Yes, that. But on the condition it will never

happen again. If it does, we will be forced to construct a wall at the arroyo."

Monty said, "What is it with you people and walls?"

Art snapped back. "What is it with you people and rockets?"

"Gentlemen," said Fran evenly. "This will get us nowhere. Monty, can we agree that you will investigate and report back at our next meeting?"

"I can ask the Abdullahs. Maybe they know something. Or maybe they know nothing like the Jews."

"Monty," cautioned Fran.

"Okay, okay."

Monty drove to the Abdullahs. They welcomed him into the doublewide and brought tea. As it was Sunday, the entire family was at home and seated together in the cramped living area. After Monty had doctored his drink, Halim asked to what they owed the honor of his visit.

"First," said Monty, "I must tell you there are neighbors."

"Neighbors? Where?" asked Halim.

"Far away. Across the arroyo on a large tract of land. A thousand acres, give or take."

Halim emitted a low whistle. "They must be

very wealthy to own such land."

"A dentist from Houston. I guess he has made some money."

Hessa spoke. "It is nice to have a neighbor."

Monty sipped his tea. "Well, yes and no. Yes, because this is isolated country and it's good to know there are people nearby."

"And bad?" she asked.

"Well . . . they're . . . Jewish. But I drove down to the arroyo before I came and you can't even see the house from your land. It's like they aren't even there."

"But Jews? Next door?" Halim buried his face in his hands.

"They won't cause problems," Monty said with a confidence he didn't feel. "You have my word. But I need to ask about something that happened a few days ago. Do you know anything about some rockets being fired across the arroyo?"

Najair spoke up. "I shot some bottle rockets down there."

Monty smiled. "Bottle rockets? Like Fourth of July?"

Halim turned to his son. "Do you have any left?"

Najair made a quick trip to his room, returning

with a package of six bottle rockets. "I almost shot these too, but then I decided to save them for a holiday."

Monty reached for them. "May I borrow these? I'll bring them back, but I need them for a certain meeting I'll be going to."

Halim started to respond, but at that moment a window pane shattered, spraying glass over them. They all ducked instinctively.

"What was that?" Halim shouted, urging everyone to the floor with hand gestures. They waited five minutes, and when no other sound came, Monty and Halim stood cautiously to examine the damage.

"Looks like a bullet hole," said Monty.

Halim said, "Here is where it went through," pointing to a small hole in an opposite window. "It is the Jew. They are trying to kill us."

"I will call the sheriff," said Monty. "And then I will demand an emergency session with Miss Fran."

Chapter 31

Ed and Wing Tour Centerfield

Ed, anxious to show off his town, took Wing on an extended tour. Beginning at the Sentinel's offices, they drove down Main Street, which had not yet been renamed Bustamonte Avenue, although a healthy percentage of the populous viewed such a change as inevitable. With Ed's own brand of commentary, he pointed out City Hall ("We're growing so fast it needs to get bigger real quick"); the newest Golden Glop ("You might want to avoid that place"); George's funeral home ("You may also want to avoid that place"); the television station ("Still waiting for those Amos and Andy re-runs"); Centerfield Elementary School ("If you visit you'll need to take a gun"); a Chinese take-out called Wok & Roll ("Don't look at me that way; I didn't name it"); a just-opened Dancing Doughnut ("That ambulance is parked outside for a reason"); the North Pole ("Everyone loves Christmas"); the First, Second, Third and Fourth Baptist Churches ("No man ever accused those Bible thumpers of originality"); Wal-more ("A necessary evil, if you ask me"); Murphy's Muffler ("A gal named Tricksy Faye used to play with his exhaust pipe back in high school").

They ended the tour at the country club. By now it was late afternoon, with the sun beginning to set. As they drove up the tree-lined serpentine drive leading to the clubhouse, Ed described it as, "My second home, but come to think of it, I spend more time here than my first home." He introduced her to his golfing buddies, suffering their sly winks and subtle elbows. All were cordial if restrained. All but one: Galen Hardwick, who had lost his collection agency business to a company in India. When introduced to Wing, Hardwick just stared.

Ed said, "Galen, where are your manners?"

"I don't like Indians," Hardwick said.

"Dots or feathers?" asked Ed.

"Dots. The feathered ones run a clean casino, but them dots steal jobs."

Ed said, "I cannot help but point out that Wing, Miss Wu, has no dot on her forehead. And there is a very good reason for that. She is not Indian."

"She's from over there, ain't she?"

"If by 'over there' you mean the Eastern Hemisphere, yes."

"Don't make no never mind to me. She's a fur-in-ner."

Ed turned to Wing, his usually genial face registering irritation and his tone purposely grave. "You must excuse Brother Galen. His ancestors swung from trees and ate bananas. Several of his uncles live in our zoo."

Wing spoke. "I agree with Mr. Galen. Indians terrible. Take jobs from China. Worship cows. Nothing stupider than a cow unless someone who worships one."

Galen raised his eyes into perfect ovals. "Say, I'm beginning to like this here gook you brought home, Ed. Mind if I show her the men's locker room?"

Ed did not reply, taking Wing gently by the arm and steering her away from the crowd that had collected around them. He ushered her to his personal golf cart. "Don't pay any attention to Galen," he said. "On the surface he's a jerk, but deep down he's an idiot."

Ed maneuvered the cart over the hills and undulations he knew so well. Some sprinklers came on as they passed the third hole. "I love this course," he said. "By this time of day, I'm usually in the clubhouse knocking down a scotch, but I need to come out here more often after the boys have finished their rounds. If I stop long enough to think about heaven, this is what I picture. Some gently rolling hills with a tricky little dogleg as you approach the green."

Wing smiled. "You a poet, Mr. Ed."

Ed shook his head. "Not much poetry in this cowboy. The way I've been living these past few years, I 'spect I should be spending more time thinking about hell than heaven."

"You think about hell?"

"Sometimes."

"What hell look like?"

Ed paused. "Knee high grass in the fairways, baked out greens with sand traps on three sides and pin placement at the top of a seven degree incline. How about you? You think about heaven and hell?"

"No. Heaven here. Hell, too."

"Yeah, that just might be the case. Were you serious when you said you want to learn to play golf?"

"For sure."

"That's my gal. How's about some lessons starting tomorrow?"

"I like that. You want one lesson or two?"

Ed cut his eyes toward her, grinning. "Competitive little thing, aren't you. This should be fun."

Chapter 32

Scott Sees a Shrink

Scott grew so depressed following his rude rejection by Miscellaneous Problems Anonymous that he sought psychiatric counseling, not so much for his fetish but for the angst caused by the 12-steppers. His first appointment with Dr. Salazar was on a Thursday.

Dr. Salazar: Scott, may I call you Scott?

Scott: Of course. And I should call you . . .?

Dr. Salazar: Joan. So Scott, your insurance plan reimburses up to eight sessions, so let's get started. What's on your mind?

Scott related the disastrous effort to address his orthopediphia in a public setting.

Joan: And how did that make you feel?

Scott: How did getting booed by a room full of people while they hissed and moved away from me holding their noses make me feel?

Joan: Yes.

Scott: Bad.

Joan: That's good. It means you are able to embrace your humiliation. You own it, so now we can deal with it. Tell me about your mother.

Scott: She's a bit on the daffy side, but she means well.

Joan: And your father?

Scott: A captain of capitalism. Funerals, death. Makes a lot of money.

Joan: And your fetish. Do you really think it's about women's orthopedic shoes?

Scott: What else?

Joan: Well, surely you have noticed that the words 'shoe' and 'sex' begin with the same letter.

Scott: So . . .

Joan: Often we project our interest in the desired, in this case sex, onto a seemingly unrelated object, in your case orthopedic shoes.

Scott: You're saying my shoe fetish is about sex?

Joan: Everything is about sex.

Scott: So why am I projecting my interest in sex onto unrelated objects like shoes?

Joan: I don't give answers here. It is up to you to discover that with my help. I merely suggest possibilities, like perhaps your sexual lusts are taboos. Homosexual, perhaps?

Scott (chuckling): That's a thought. I can't wait to tell Allison about it. That's my girlfriend. We've been projecting since we were fifteen.

Joan: Your mother, perhaps? Some oedipal issue that needs attention?

Scott: Now there's a creepy thought.

Joan: That's my job, Scott. To raise what you call creepy thoughts that you've otherwise suppressed.

Scott (sighing): Look Joan, I have no desires, suppressed or otherwise, where my mother is concerned, God love her. If I had any interest in bonking within the family, I had a very hot sister right down the hall.

Joan: Now we are making progress. I see our time is up. Next time we will explore your relationship with your hot sister.

Scott (skeptical): How long will that take?

Joan: About seven more sessions.

Chapter 33

Buster Lives Down to
Fran's Low Expectations

Fran attended a special meeting at the town hall called by Mayor Buster. Judging by those attending, it could have been mistaken for a Bustamonte family reunion. Present were Ernesto Bustamonte, Hector Bustamonte, Jorge "Speedy" Bustamonte, Rosalinda Bustamonte, Ronaldo Bustamonte, etc.

The announced purpose of the meeting was to review preliminary design plans for the Centerfield Park. Mayor Buster began by introducing the design team from Rios, Chavez and Bustamonte, after which the lead designer, Carlos Rios, asked that the lights be dimmed as he positioned himself at a laptop computer. On a pull-down screen, an aerial view of the park came into focus. He froze the image over soccer and baseball fields, outdoor picnic areas, a petting zoo, a botanical garden, an amphitheater, a rodeo ring, an indoor arcade with a food court patio. After a chorus of oohs and aahs died down, he reminded those present that the scope and reach of the amenities very much depended on the size of the land parcel set aside for the park. The minimum area to accommodate the plan they had just seen was forty acres; ideal would be seventy-five. He opened the floor for questions.

Fran raised her hand. "You have shown us some impressive infrastructure. What about the exterior?"

Rios said, "Glad you asked. We have some very preliminary sketches I'll show you now. A fine park like this needs an imposing entrance. Our hope is that the entrance will front on or at the end of a major access point, like a divided avenue well landscaped." He hit a few keystrokes, after which a frontal and side view appeared on the screen.

Fran asked, "What is that column in front of the entrance?"

"A pedestal. The mayor suggested a statue could be placed there as a fitting welcome to visitors."

Fran glanced at Buster, who avoided eye contact with a mayoral stare over the audience, a guilty plea to the charge he had borrowed her suggestion without attribution.

"And now," said Rios, "a few words from the mayor."

Buster bowed to enthusiastic applause. "Thank you for coming today. I am sure you are as impressed as I am by the wonderful design we have just seen. Of course, I would like to see more bezzball fields . . ." (general laughter) "but seriously, this park would be a good thing for our city. As you know, I believe in good things so I will do everything I can to see that this park is built."

Fran couldn't resist. "Mr. Mayor, have you given any thought to whose statue might welcome visitors to the park?"

Buster actually blushed. "Well, no, I have been too busy with my official duties to give that detail any thought at all. Of course, it needs to be someone well known, with a reputation for extraordinary accomplishment. It should be someone with a long history here in Centerfield, a person who has been important to the growth of the town. Because our community is somewhat new as Texas towns go, it should be a living person. And because we will want people from all over the country and the world to visit our park, it should be someone known throughout the world. Possibly someone who honors our close ties with our neighbor Mexico."

Fran suppressed a grin. "But other than that, you've given the matter no thought."

Chapter 34

Monty confronts Art
over the rifle shot

The emergency convocation in *The Sentinel's* Conference Room A pitted a morally outraged Monty against a curious Art. Fran hadn't even opened the meeting when Monty threw onto the table the package of bottle rockets Najair had loaned him. "Here is your terrorist weapon," he hissed at Art. "A harmless bottle rocket that wouldn't hurt a grasshopper."

"It is the principle," said Art calmly after a moment to recover. "I don't have to tell you the significance of rockets fired into our territory."

"Child's play," said Monty, "fired by a child, an eight-year-old boy who had no idea anyone was living across the arroyo."

"Ah!" said Art. "So you had not informed your settlers that Jews lived next door?"

"They know now," said Monty, "and your settlers, the Levys, clearly know of the Abdullahs because they tried to kill them."

Fran spoke for the first time. "What

happened?"

"A rifle bullet was fired into their home. I was there at the time. No one was hurt, but we were all terrified. The children won't leave the house to play. The sheriff came but didn't learn anything."

"That is obviously very serious. What makes you think the Levys are responsible?"

Monty scoffed. "Because they are Jews, and Jews always retaliate. This was payback for a few harmless bottle rockets."

Fran turned to Art. "Well?"

Art shook his head. "It wasn't the Levys. I've been to their home many times and they are not the kind of people who would do such a thing."

"Do they own a rifle?" Fran asked.

"Two, I think. Anyone who lives in the middle of a thousand acres of rural Texas would own a gun. Probably several."

"Did the sheriff question them?" Fran asked.

"I doubt it," said Monty in a sulk.

"Because?"

"Because they probably paid him off with all their money."

Fran pointedly cleared her throat. "I've known Sheriff Butler for years. He can't be bought. Could it have been a hunter?"

Monty hesitated long enough to confirm this as a possibility he had not considered.

Art said, "Chaim hasn't mentioned anyone looking for permission to hunt the place, but I can ask him."

Monty subjected Art to some piercing eye contact. "I'm going to find that bullet if it takes ten years. And when I do, I'm going to get it matched up against the Levys' rifles. Shooting into an occupied house is a felony. I checked."

Art sighed skeptically. "There is an innocent explanation. I'm certain of it."

I'm not," Monty replied. "If it happens again we may be forced to take matters into our own hands. The next rockets may be larger."

"You see?" Art said to Fran. "What begins small can escalate."

"What I see," she said, "is two men who distrust each other over grievances as old as time. In the immortal words of Rodney King, 'can't we all just get along?'"

"No," said Monty.

"No," said Art.

Chapter 35

Joyce stresses over
Shawn Pen's visit

Joyce's determination to host Shawn Pen on his visit to Centerfield was tempered by the ugly fact that access to the Fafalone home was still impeded by the pit. Every time she closed her eyes to envision it--a stretch limo gliding smoothly through the front gate before coming to a stop at her front door, a crisply uniformed chauffeur walking briskly to the rear door, opening it with a muted flourish, cameras clicking as Shawn exited with the practiced nonchalance of a true star, his manly stride up her walk on the red carpet she would have custom made for the occasion, her restrained exuberance at the top of the stairway, where she waited with a spray of roses and a bottle of mineral water--every time she saw in her mind's eye that scene as surely as if it was happening at that very moment, the pit loomed to spoil it. It simply would not do to have Shawn walk around the pit through the mesquite trees. The problem presented by the pit simply must be solved, she told George as he munched on a brownie.

George reminded her that the pit was as much an inconvenience to him as to anyone, that he also wanted it repaired, and that technically it was far from certain that Shawn would be staying in their home, a caution brushed aside by Joyce as more of George's pessimism. In fact, she had engaged their architect, Dwight LaCalle, to remodel the guest room, ordered a new king size bed, and framed the posters for every film Shawn had made to be displayed on the remodeled walls. She told George with uncharacteristic firmness that Shawn **would** be staying there, that she intended to spend whatever amount of money was required to make his visit memorable, and that she did not care about the wolf at the door.

"My surgery is a few weeks before that," he said.

"Well I should hope so," she said. "Everyone in Hollywood is thin except for the people who put up the money. I want you to be thin, too. That liposuction couldn't come at a better time."

George finished his Brownie, brushed his hands together to rid them of residual crumbs and said, "It's not just liposuction, you know. I decided if I'm going under the ether I should go all the way."

"So what else?"

"Stomach staples, so I won't gain the weight back. And knee replacement."

"Which one?"

"Both. And I'll get the hernia fixed. And those hemorrhoids that have been bothering me."

"Isn't that a lot for one surgery? You'll be in the hospital a long time."

"Not really. The insurance company called it outpatient. I had to fight like hell to get them to pay for an overnight."

"Well, in that case you will be a new man by the time Shawn arrives. What are we going to do about that pit?"

"I'll talk with Fran again. She has the worst of it with all the dust so near her house."

Chapter 36

The mud wrestling contest

Art adopted a philosophic view of Tricky's time at the North Pole. Having seen her performance, he now appreciated it in ways he could never have envisioned. What she did on Friday nights demanded stamina, flexibility and athleticism, not to mention patience with all the leering cowboys who wanted to reach for more than their five dollars entitled them to. But most of the gawkers were harmless, Art realized; hard working good ole boys who liked to drink a few brews and admire the female form. He could hardly fault them there, having himself admired that form from the day he met her at the county courthouse. Art appreciated Tricky's dedication to her work, and of course the flood of $1's and $5's she brought home helped, too.

Reverend Klingenpeal, owner of the North Pole, also appreciated Tricksy. She brought in more customers who stayed longer and consumed more beer than any other dancer he employed. His cash flow rose and fell in direct relationship to her time on the pole. Which is why he decided to sponsor the first mud wrestling contest in the history of Centerfield.

Tricksy debated telling Art about Klingenpeal's latest entrepreneurial brainstorm. Chances were good he would never find out about it, and why disturb his comfort level with her work by injecting some new variable that could be considered moderately distasteful by those with limited vision. But in the end, she opted for honesty.

"Art, honey, old man Klingenpeep (she called him that when at home) has come up with a new moneymaker."

"Selling kosher hot dogs? I suggested that to him."

"No, what he's selling ain't kosher, whatever that is. As usual, it's me."

"More dancing?"

"Not exactly. You remember Lucinda from down at the club?"

"Is she the one with the very large--"

"Yeah, that's the one. But they are implants so in my book they don't count. Anyway, Klingenpeep has ordered a indoor swimming pool. He's going to fill it with mud and get me and Lucinda to wrestle in it. He says the price of a ringside seat will be $100."

"He wants you to wrestle in mud? How strange."

"Well see, we just wear t-shirts and thongs. It is not the most dignified thing you've ever seen. But he's paying big money and he is my boss so I guess I'll go through with it. The winner gets a trophy, but that ain't the most dignified thing you've ever seen either. I don't know where you would display such a thing."

"Over the fireplace?"

"Lucinda is going down. That I can promise, even though she outweighs me by twenty pounds because of them implants."

"Have you ever wrestled before?"

"Not in mud. How will I ever get that stuff out of my hair, not to mention other places where mud ain't supposed to go. I'll need to walk through a car wash after it's over."

"I am sorry, Tricksy, but I have to draw the mark."

"You mean draw the line?"

"I have to draw the line at you walking through a car wash. What will people say?"

"You win, Arttie. No car wash."

.

Chapter 37

Dirty Todd Melville Comes Clean

In her office at *The Sentinel*, Fran answered a call from the very last person she wanted or expected to hear from: Todd Melville.

"So, Todd," she said, "how is the Mrs.?"

"Fran, I can explain."

"And you can lie. I believe we can agree on that?"

"I was less than honest, yes."

"There was a time that was known as lying."

"I don't blame you for being angry."

"Then you misjudge me. I got over my anger in about twenty minutes."

"That isn't a very long time."

"It's double what you deserved. Speaking of time, I'm on a deadline. How may I help you?"

"I'm coming to Centerfield. I was hoping we could meet for coffee."

"I don't think so."

"Please, Fran, everyone deserves another chance. To show you how much I want this meeting, I'm willing to send you a check for $5000. I know you won't take the money, but just name a charity and I'll make it out to them."

"Five thousand dollars for coffee?"

"Yes."

She hesitated. "That sounds a bit crazy, Todd, but if you're serious make it out to the Boys and Girls Club of Centerfield. Call me back when the check clears."

The following day, an overnight envelope arrived with a Dallas return address. Inside was a certified check drawn on SNEEZE, the Society for New Ethical Enlightenment with Zen Emphasis. A week later, she met Todd Melville for coffee.

Over lattes, Todd said, "You look great."

"As do you," she said, and she meant it. "Thank you for the check. It will help bridge a budget gap at the club. They were thrilled to get it."

"My pleasure. As I said on the phone, I wanted this meeting to explain our previous miscommunication."

"Todd, if you want to talk, as you say you do, let's get something straight. You told me you were divorced and in fact you were married. That small technicality is what you are now describing as your being 'less than honest' and a 'previous miscommunication.' It seems to me that any discussion ought to begin with a confession closer to 'I lied.'"

"You are right. I lied. I did it to get you in bed."

"Now we're getting somewhere. From what I've heard, that bed was pretty crowded."

"Most women I meet are, shall we say, less resistant than you were."

"Too bad for them."

"But I've changed."

"Let me guess. You really are divorced, you can prove it, and now you want to pick up where we left off."

The pained smile that formed on his lips told Fran she was dead wrong. He said, "As pleasant as that thought is to me, the truth is that my wife, Nan Tucker, and I have truly reconciled, and I no longer find it necessary to roam like some stray tomcat."

Fran, her blush of embarrassment beginning to fade, said, "I'm happy for you both."

After an awkward silence, during which both stared down into their coffee cups, Todd said, "I hardly recognize Centerfield. The place is booming. By the way, I still read *The Sentinel*."

She smiled. "I knew there was something I liked about you. Yes, we seem to be growing. Too fast for our own good, I often think."

"Whatever happened to Father Richards? Is he still doing the Lord's work at COUGH?"

Fran squinted into the distance. "The last I heard he had taken a sabbatical to do some missionary work in Haiti."

Todd said, "I was disappointed you lost the election. You would have made a great mayor."

"Thank you. I may still get the chance. Buster is coming up for reelection and a lot of folks want a change. I've been approached by a number of the town's leaders to try again."

"That is a nice segue into the reason I wanted to meet with you."

"I was wondering when we would get to that."

He said, "I've had calls from some of those leaders you mentioned. Despite my reputation as a philanderer—a reputation I hope is fading—there are people here I still call friends. They want my support if they can persuade you to run."

"In other words, money."

"It's more than money. Fran, this country is in a crisis. It's being run by two political parties that can't sit down to talk over a free lunch. They take strong stands on minor issues and delay the major decisions to the day when they will have absolute power. When that day comes, they won't have to compromise, but of course that day never has or will come, so they are living in a fantasy political universe while the country slides toward the sewer."

"Well said, and so true."

"Which is why, after much study and introspection, I've joined forces with Texas First."

"The secessionist outfit?"

"Circulating those secession petitions is only part of the agenda. The real mission is to take back the government and put it into the hands of people who are pragmatic problem solvers. People like you. State and national politics are the magnets for all the egos that created this mess. Winning a governorship or a Congressional seat is almost impossible because of all the money that flows to the major party candidates. It is local office, like the mayor of Centerfield, where real opportunity lies. If we can elect enough people to town councils and school boards and the like, we can take back Texas from the bottom up."

"What makes you think that the people you elect won't turn into the people you want to get rid of?"

"Frannie, you always manage to go to the heart of the matter. That is the issue. And the answer, the only answer, is to recruit the candidates who believe in the mission; who believe the goal is more important than any one political career."

"In other words, candidates willing to take one for the team."

"At the risk of waxing poetic, candidates willing to take one for the dream."

"Why Todd, that is downright inspiring."

"Thanks. Rehearsed that line driving down."

"I can't pretend I'm not interested. Buster is a good person, but he treats the office of mayor like it is another Hall of Fame, where they display a bust for past achievements. Centerfield needs a progressive leader."

"Like you."

"I learned a lot in losing to him last time. I think I can win, but I have to weigh the opportunity against my obligations to the paper and my kids."

"I have full confidence you'll make the right decision, and when you do I'll help raise the money. I hope you aren't going to again insist on that silly one-hundred-dollar limit per contributor."

"What do you think?"

"Okay. One hundred it is."

"And Todd, just so there is no confusion here, I think the movement to have Texas secede is about as wacky an idea as anything out there."

Chapter 38

Fran vs. Buster, Round 2

Did she REALLY want to run for mayor again?
Fran resisted serious and prolonged introspection.
She always had. She operated more by instinct, a
biological gyroscope she relied on to point her, if not
true north, at least north-by-something close. She
knew people who listed pro's and con's--literally set
them down in competing columns as if life's
decisions could mirror double-entry bookkeeping,
with the final computation a destiny-freighted debit
or credit. She thought of this method as sophisticated
witchcraft, a gimmick to convince the witch she had
considered all the angles and had arrived at that
most prized decision: informed. Listing positives and
negatives was, in Fran's view, useless unless you
assigned a weight to each. For example, the decision
to send your kids to private school could be resisted
by an army of con's: expensive, elitist, narrowing,
racist; but when balanced against the one
indisputable con for public schools, that they
SUCKED and your kid was likely to graduate high
school reading at a fourth grade level, the only

question left was where to send your check. Fortunately for her, the public schools in Centerfield, while flawed, did not suck. And, as mayor, she could work to improve them. Something in her gut rather than a tally on a scorecard told her she should do this.

She called together Chip, Sarah and James for a family meeting. She told them she was weighing another run for mayor, that the campaign would require her to spend time away from home, that if she won a significant amount of her time would have to be devoted to the city's business, and that such time would, on occasion, come at their expense. She said they would always be her first priority, but she thought it fair to let them know what was at stake. She asked for their questions or concerns.

Sarah wanted to know if she would be called Mrs. Mayor.

"That is an excellent question, Sarah. I'm sure I will be called many things, not all of them pretty, but that is what politics has come to. Some citizens will call me Mrs. Mayor, and some will call me Her Honor because they call Mayor Bustamonte His Honor, even though most just call him Buster."

Sarah nodded her emphatic understanding while simultaneously reaching a prepubescent decision. "I will call you Mayor Mom."

James said he thought it was a good idea, that she owed Buster one for her loss to him earlier, and wondered if it might offer him an opportunity to meet girls from schools other than his own, all of which brought a pasty if indulgent frown from his mother.

"Revenge is no reason to run," she said.

"Ah, c'mon Mom, don't you want to kick a little Bustamonte butt?"

Fran lips began to spread in a visceral smile before she reined it in. "I'd like to think of it as redemption."

"Fine," said James. "You can redeem a little Bustamonte butt."

Chip said he planned to be off at college so therefore not directly affected, but he thought it would be good for the city. Fran smiled at that and thanked him. Then Chip added, "And I'm with James. The guy needs to be taken down."

Next, she met with Ed, whom she hardly recognized as the same man since meeting Wing. Not only had his drinking habits become more restrained, but he could no longer be counted upon to hit on every woman wearing a skirt, dress, slacks, shorts, or burka. His main preoccupation seemed to be teaching Wing golf, and from what Fran had heard, Wing was catching on quickly.

They met in Fran's office with the door closed. She told him she wanted to get his feelings about a run for Buster's job. Ed chuckled and said she knew damn well she had his full support, that he would actively campaign for her, and that to show how much he wanted her to win, he wouldn't even demand she sleep with him. Fran chuckled at that; maybe the old Ed wasn't gone after all.

"My one concern is *The Sentinel*," she said. "As you know, I've been exploring the possibility of making us an on-line newspaper."

Ed shook his head from side to side slowly. "My daddy would roll over in his grave . . ."

"If we don't change with the times, Ed, we'll all be in an economic grave. I'm afraid it's inevitable. Look at all the papers that are closing. Printing and distribution are simply too expensive."

"Oh, I know it," he said. "I just don't like it. Seems like everything is moving so fast. But I trust you to make some good decisions for us."

"Well, that's just it. I feel capable of handling the changes, but if I become the mayor I will be stretched pretty thin."

"My daddy always said that if you want

something done, give it to someone who is busy. I believe that. You can handle it."

"I appreciate the vote of confidence. If I win, I intend to relinquish any role in the editorial policy. Every city government needs a newspaper looking over its shoulder, so someone will need to be looking over mine."

"Kirstin?"

"Yes. She's ready. She grows in her job by the month."

He nodded. "Impressive young woman, I have to say. We're lucky to have her."

"And I want to keep her, which is why I'm going to need to give her a big raise. Is that okay with you, boss?"

"Frannie, as long as I can pay the bills, sip some good single malt scotch, keep Wing supplied with golf lessons and designer clothes, I'm a happy man. Pay her whatever we need to pay."

"Good. I thought you would say that. And will you help me raise some money for this race? It is likely to be expensive."

"Will you finally go to bed with me? You know, just for old times sake."

"Yes, I will," Fran said.

Ed's eyebrows shot up. "You will?"

"Yes. I've decided it is high time to find out just how good a lover you are."

Ed coughed. "Well, I . . ."

"There is only one condition," Fran added. "I want Wing there, too."

"Won't that be awkward? You and me in the sack together and Wing right next door?"

"Who said anything about next door?"

"You mean . . . with us? The three of us together?"

"For God's sake, Ed, it's the twenty-first century."

"I have a feeling Wing isn't going to buy into that. And I'm a bit old fashioned myself."

"That's too bad. And just when I thought we might have our time together."

"You're a cruel woman, Fran, to play with me like that."

She laughed and stood up. "You deserve every bit of it, as you know. I'll let you know what Kirstin says when I speak with her."

Chapter 39

FEMA Arrives, and There Goes the Neighborhood

After the shot was fired through the Abdullahs' living room window, the family discussed leaving. For Halim and Hessa, the safety of their children came before the free land and open skies of New P. But Najair and Rayya resisted the idea of returning to Detroit and assured their parents that they felt no more at risk than children living in Gaza or the West Bank, which their tutor was educating them on along with the Bible lessons in Christianity. They felt like pioneers, they told their parents, who were proud of such maturity. What they really wanted, the children said, was some friends like the ones they had left in Detroit. Halim and Hessa shared this longing, for as much as they liked the endless space they enjoyed in New P, and as much as each enjoyed the job they commuted to and the home they came back to, they too were lonely for "people like us."

The Abdullahs' desire for Arab neighbors fit perfectly into Monty's plan to populate New P. The problem was housing. He had scrambled to find the trailer the Abdullahs occupied and in fact was still paying rent on it that was only partly offset by what the Abdullahs paid him. How could he recruit new citizens to a place with no housing for them?

Then he read an article in *The Sentinel* about thousands of FEMA trailers sitting unused in some giant parking lot. The article disclosed negotiations between FEMA and the Defense Department, which wanted to purchase the trailers as targets for some top-secret drone technology being developed for deployment in Pakistan and Afghanistan. The article went on to say that air quality testing on the trailers had shown unacceptable levels of formaldehyde, making them unfit for human occupation, and that their use as targets was a last resort to dumping them off Florida to become coral reefs.

Monty drove to San Antonio, where he found an inventory of trailers that seemed to stretch for miles. A FEMA rep named Clyde Sisk met him there.

Monty: "So, how much do you want for the trailers?"

Clyde: "One hundred dollars apiece."

Monty: "Is that all?"

Clyde: "That's it. We offer financing too."

Monty: "Doesn't the government lose a lot of money on a deal like that?"

Clyde: "It's nothing compared to the hit we took when we paid the manufacturers for equipping them with formaldehyde."

Monty: "So formaldehyde is a problem?"

Clyde: "Only if you plan to live in it, which you cannot do under the terms of sale."

Monty: "How do you know I won't live in it?"

Clyde: "You have to sign a waiver acknowledging that you have been told about the dangers of formaldehyde and promising not to live in it."

Monty: "So I promise and that's it?"

Clyde: "That's it. Between you and me, I think these puppies are safe. I live in one myself."

Monty: "But the formaldehyde . . ."

Clyde: "Some EPA summer intern did the study that resulted in the warning. He locked four hundred mice in one and a few died. I'm guessing those few were allergic to formaldehyde. Everyone is allergic to something."

Monty: "So I pay you $100, sign the waiver, drive the trailer off and that's the end of it as far as FEMA is concerned."

Clyde: "You got it."

Monty: "I'll take fifty."

Clyde: "Good decision. You want to select the

one you buy?"

    Monty: "Aren't they all the same?"

    Clyde: "Down to the last rivet."

    Monty: "Then I'll pass."

    Clyde: "Another good decision. Well, shall we get started on the paperwork? You need to lock in the deal before the Defense Department gets here on Friday."

    It took Monty a week of commuting back and forth to San Antonio to get all fifty trailers to Centerfield. He spaced them evenly throughout New P, selecting one as the model. For $12 he purchased some plastic picket fencing at Wal-more and for another $25 some outdoor carpet for landscaping. The photo and ad he ran in the *Detroit Free Press* brought hundreds of inquiries. A month later, New P boasted of fifty new Arab families and an overnight population of 381.

Chapter 40

Art and Monty Honor the Second Principle of Negotiations

The arrival of 377 more Arabs from Detroit caused major consternation in New I's Jewish community, primarily because that community still consisted of Chaim Levy and his wife. When Levy learned that fifty newly occupied FEMA trailers now dotted the New P landscape, he shared his worries with Art.

"It is one thing to have a single Arab family like the Abdullahs, who have not met me but whom I feel certain hate me with all their being, but it is quite another thing to have my property bordered by a ghetto of transplanted Detroit Palestinians."

Art reacted defensively. "I have increased the Yiddish ads in Houston and Dallas and have expanded them to Fort Worth and Austin. Where are the sons and daughters of Zion when we need them?"

"The problem," said Chaim, "is the uncertainty of the land titles. Very few of our people will do what I did, which is to make a large investment in property we may never own. At the risk of tooting my own flute, that takes chutzpah, and a giant set of cojones, which I happen to have."

Art realized this was true, and he privately hoped Chaim would never mention to Tricksy anything regarding his large cojones for fear her curiosity would get the better of her. "I am aware," he said, "of the title problem, and doing my best in negotiations to resolve it."

"What is the status of those negotiations?" asked Chaim.

"As you can imagine, Monty demands concessions."

"So?"

"It is the first principle of negotiations that no concessions can be made."

"Is Monty willing to give concessions?"

"No."

"Why?"

"He must have attended the same school of negotiation that I did, as he says the first principle of negotiations that no concessions can be made."

"You will pardon my dullness, but this sounds like Republicans negotiating with Democrats. How is any progress to be made?"

"It is true that we seem to be going nowhere at a rapid rate. Even Fran, who has a pasture of patience, is getting discouraged."

"Surely there is some concession that could be made. Perhaps if you gave a small concession, Monty could be induced to give a larger one. What is it he wants?"

"Immediate death to all Jews."

"I think we can agree that is not a small concession. There must be something else."

"He complains often about the checkpoints we plan to build that will assure that the papers of Arabs coming to work in New I are in order."

Chaim raised a pointed finger of inspiration. "Aha! There is a possible concession. There is no work for Arabs in New I, so no need for checkpoints. It is the second principle of negotiation that giving up something that you don't want or need is shrewd bargaining."

Art rubbed his chin. "I don't know. I like checkpoints. They make me feel . . . secure."

"But you don't even live there, and I do. I am okay without checkpoints. Why don't you offer that as a concession and see how Monty responds? Maybe he will make a reasonable but larger concession, like sending all those Arabs back to Detroit."

Art pledged to see what could be done, and at the next session with Fran, he surprised both Fran and Monty by stating that he had come prepared to make a concession. Fran smiled appreciatively while Monty folded his arms and scowled, muttering something about a Zionist trick.

Art was the picture of diplomacy when he said, "I have taken seriously the complaints about plans to build checkpoints in New I. Today, after consultation with the great Zionist movement, I renounce these plans. There will be no checkpoints in the foreseeable future."

Fran turned to Monty. "This has been a constant complaint of yours, Monty. Do you have a concession to make to Art? A concession should be matched, don't you think?"

Monty unfolded his arms and leaned on the table. "I agree that a concession should be matched. In reply, I will agree to send back to Detroit every one of our new citizens of New P that belongs to Hummus."

Art stared at him coldly. "You have people on the border of New I that belong to that terrorist organization?"

"Of course not. That is why I agreed to send them back. I too believe in the second principle of negotiation."

"Gentlemen," said Fran, "I respectfully ask you

both to make a mutual and meaningful concession. Art, I ask that you renounce checkpoints now and in the future. Permanently. Forever. And Monty, I want you to pledge that no member of Hummus will ever be allowed to settle in New P."

Art and Monty looked down as if studying the grain of wood in the conference table. Then Art said, "I will agree if he agrees."

Monty said, "And I will agree if he agrees."

"Then we are agreed," Fran said. "Same time next week?"

Chapter 41

Joyce Earns her Spurs
With SPHINCTER

Joyce's elevation to the TCP (Truly Caring Person) level of SPHINCTER gave her access to the email addresses of other members in her area. She contacted each one. A Facebook page devoted to the group assured that no one would miss any Shawn news, Shawn sightings, or Shawn rumors. Each member of the group could be counted on to "like" every post by another member, even if that post was a grandmother's recipe for orange marmalade that no one had actually made in half a century.

Joyce hosted a garden party, where topics of conversation numbered exactly one: Shawn's impending visit. His publicist had provided a firm date: October 24 and 25. No itinerary had yet been released, but a SPHINCTER website posting confirmed he would be spending the night. Joyce resolved that his night would be spent at the Fafalone residence. In the meantime, members had been asked to propose projects worthy of Shawn's compassion. Naturally, Joyce served as the clearinghouse for such proposals. After collecting and studying them, she ranked them in no particular order of worthiness.

The Armadillo Speed Bump Project. On a stretch of highway leading into Centerfield, an unusually large number of roadkill armadillos had been verified between mile markers 71 and 72. Local PETA proposed speed bumps at the mile markers. Joyce initially ranked this high until George pointed out that the speed limit along that road was 75 m.p.h., and that a car hitting a bump at that speed would be launched fifteen feet into the air. "Also," he predicted, "you'll have more dead motorcyclists than armadillos."

The Unloved Books Initiative. Proposed by the Library Guild, which surveyed the local library and identified 28,751 books that had never been checked out. The proposal suggested that the names of all registered voters in Centerfield be put into a hopper, and that Shawn would pick out 28,751 names, the assumption being that anyone personally selected by Mr. Pen himself would be willing to read one unloved book with a view to ranking it as (1) boring; (2) very boring; and (3) excruciatingly boring. The flaw identified here was the realization that withdrawing 28,751 names would require eleven days if Mr. Pen neither ate nor slept.

The Orphan Silent Auction: Centerfield possessed one small orphanage with a current population of twenty-two. At a gala event to be hosted by Shawn, each orphan would stand by a station set up for bidding. The town's glamoratzie, urged by Shawn and an extended cocktail hour to open their hearts and wallets, would gradually bid the orphans up and up, raising some serious money that could be put either toward the winning orphan's college fund or, should the winning bid prove more modest, a day trip for all the orphans to a larger orphanage in Austin.

The Cleopatra Competition: A little known key to her legendary beauty was a perfectly formed head, discovered when she shaved it as a young woman to prove her love for a suitor, Neiman Marcus. The contest contemplated all women in Centerfield willing to shave their heads would have those heads massaged by a blindfolded Shawn, who would select the most perfectly shaped among them.

The "Adopt an Indian Landfill" Initiative. This idea sprang from the mind of a local SPHINCTERette who had found herself profoundly influenced by the film Slumdog Millionaire. For one city to "adopt" a foreign one as a sister city had by now become an accepted method to recognize the world's increasing interdependence, but this took that concept a giant step further by Centerfield's sponsorship of a landfill in Mumbai to be selected by Mr. Pen after a tour of the available locations. Each participating Centerfielder would receive a photograph and a letter from a child living on the landfill. In turn, the recipient would send his or her special child a family photo, preferably taken at Christmas, and a check not to exceed $10 (to avoid spoiling the child). One obstacle to be overcome related to landfill addresses for the children, as the Indian postal service had been slow to organize mail delivery in some of the newer locations. Joyce worried that language would be a barrier until reminded that many Indians spoke English, but she herself was credited with the solution to the mailing problem with her suggestion that an abandoned school bus ("Isn't there always an abandoned school bus?" she had asked) be designated as the general delivery mailbox for all incoming communications from Centerfield.

Joyce glowed with anticipation as Shawn said, as he surely would on his arrival, that proposals like the ones she had selected was what SPHINCTER was all about.

Chapter 42

Halim makes an investment

Halim built a reputation as one of the best mechanics in Centerfield. Before long, customers needing auto repair asked for him by name and refused to let others work on their cars. But Halim nourished larger ambitions. Perhaps it was the Texas air that fueled his entrepreneurial fever, because when one of his customers mentioned that the Pack 'N Play Gun Store was for sale, he went to see the owner.

Bart Bennett had owned the Pack 'N Play for twenty years. When it opened, it was the only gun store in Centerfield. Then Wal-more arrived, taking many of the casual customers and putting the Pack 'N Play's profits at risk. Bennett decided to sell and move to Naples, Florida, where he was in the middle of building a seven thousand square foot home.

On the day Halim went to see him, Bennett was in a selling mood and Halim was equally determined to buy. During a tour of the store, Halim showed particular interest in the door that furnished customer access to the parking lot.

Bennett said, "Bulletproof, of course. And very secure. We've never had a break-in. I guess you would have to be a little crazy to try to rob a gun store, but there are folks out there who are crazy, and not just a little. It happens, but in twenty years it hasn't happened here. Which is not to say that door doesn't cost me money. Air conditioning ain't cheap, and here you need it ten months a year. Some customers hold that door open like they are trying to cool the state of Texas."

Halim said, "I know something about guns, a lot about mechanics, but little about the laws."

"The main thing is the background check."

"Is that difficult?"

"Not really. You know those orange jumpsuits they make prisoners wear?"

"I have seen them on TV."

"Okay, if a customer comes in and he is wearing one of those, there is a three-day waiting period to sell him a gun."

Halim nodded. "That makes sense. Is the waiting period required for others?"

"Absolutely," Bennett said. "Anyone comes in with their guide dog, we make 'em wait. And also for the folks speaking in tongues. We get a few of those from time to time. It's a judgment call. If they are just mumbling about Jesus, I usually let 'em slide, figuring that no one who is in touch with a higher power, in whatever language, is going to do any real damage. Every now and again we'll get somebody talking about Satan, or at least it sounds like Satan, and those you have to be careful with. Like I say, it's a judgment call."

"And the kids?"

"Best part of the job. I love it just before school opens when the kindergarteners come in to buy their first gun. They are so cute. Smart too, You'd be surprised at how much they know about calibers and fire power. Those video games are educational that way, especially that new one, Nursery Nightmare. Had a little girl in here last year that scored over eighteen thousand on that game before her fourth birthday. Most adults can't do that well."

"I'm interested," said Halim. "Can I see the books?"

"Of course. Got them right here, knowing you would want to take a look-see."

Halim studied the books, satisfied with the return on investment he would have to make to acquire the store. Bennett was offering financing, which was a plus. He talked it over with Hessa, who worried about Halim's personal safety and was reassured by Bennett's report that he had not been held up in twenty years.

"What about competition?" she asked.

"I worry about that," he admitted. "Wal-more is a serious one, and gun shops are opening everywhere. I need a draw, something that will make our store stand out from all the rest, and I think I've found one."

A month later, Halim paid Bennett most of their savings as a down payment and signed a note for the balance, secured by the store. He closed the store for a week to remodel the entrance. He had an idea that had come to him in the discussion of the front door and the loss of air conditioning. He used the rest of their savings to rip out the existing door and install a new revolving door. But it was not just a typical revolving door. He had it custom made by a company he found on the internet. Halim's door had six compartments as opposed to the usual three or four. It also had some curious indentations on each compartment. Then, above the door, he mounted a long PVC cylinder he spray painted black after installing at the end of it a metal semicircle. The completed PVC looked for all the world like the barrel of a gun, complete with sight, and it was visible from a mile away. Once customers approached the door, they realized it resembled the chamber of a pistol, so that when they entered one of the compartments, they became, in effect, a human bullet.

"Brilliant," Bennett admitted on his last visit before leaving for Naples. "Wish I'd thought of it myself. Not only will you save a ton on air conditioning, but you are psychologically priming people to buy before they set foot in the place. Damn. Why didn't I think of that?"

Chapter 43

George Meets Zorro

George returned to Dr. Malloy, who congratulated him on weighing in at 351. "This should eliminate any insurance issues," Malloy assured him.

"It was that super supreme pizza that put me over the top," George said. "Extra cheese. For a while I wasn't sure I could finish it, but I had set a goal and knew every bite was important. When can I get scheduled for the big suck."

"How much weight do you expect to be removed?"

"One hundred pounds."

Malloy rubbed his chin. "That is more weight than these procedures usually handle. In fact, only a few places in the entire country will attempt them. The closest is in Houston. The Hoover Clinic."

"Hoover is the name of the doctor?"

"No. It's owned and run by the vacuum cleaner company. Same principle, so it makes sense. I'll call them to see how soon they can get you in."

"I hope it won't be long. Joyce says I need to be

thin when Shawn Pen arrives."

Two weeks later, George arrived at the Hoover Clinic, housed on the top floor of a Houston medical complex. He and Joyce were greeted by an Asian man in a white medical coat. His name tag said "Zorro."

"My real name is Dr. Chin," he explained, "but the staff here calls me Zorro so I had this name tag made."

"Why Zorro?" Joyce asked.

"I do my work with a cannula; a suction wand. To some it reminds them of a sword. And then there is the black cape I wear while operating."

George said, "My doc back home in Centerfield said you are one of the few who will tackle a one-hundred-pound liposuction."

"That is so," said Dr. Chin. "With such a drastic weight removal, there are more risks. Many doctors are afraid of such risks, but I am Zorro. I welcome them."

Concerned, Joyce asked, "Risks such as?"

"Mostly side effects," Zorro said. "More discomfort, longer healing times, more swelling around the impacted areas; things like that. And there is increased risk from infection. But these are common with any major surgical procedure."

He took George's vital signs, then asked him to remove his shirt. "That is quite a belly you have there," said Zorro matter-of-factly. "I'll need to do some tucking while I'm at it or your skin will hang down to your knees."

"Do whatever you need to do," Joyce said. "We're hosting Shawn Pen--you know, THE Shawn Pen--in a few weeks and George wants to look his best."

Zorro smiled. "By the time I get through with him, you will have a hard time distinguishing between your husband and your guest." They set the surgery date for a week later.

On the day before the appointed day, Joyce drove George to Houston, where they spent the night to be certain to arrive on time the following morning. Surgery was scheduled for 6 a.m. George weighed in at 353. Just before he donned a XXXL surgical gown, Zorro had him stand at attention while Zorro marked the targeted areas with a blue pen.

"Just think," George said to Joyce as he lay on the industrial strength gurney, "in a few hours I'll be down to 253. I don't think I've been that light since our honeymoon."

The anesthesiologist came by, followed by Zorro himself. He wore green surgical scrubs under a black cape.

"I guess I thought you were joking about the cape," George said.

"It empowers me," said Zorro. "You want an empowered doctor for this procedure."

"You don't wear a mask, do you?"

"Oh, how I wish, but it could affect my vision. Well, are you ready?"

"Ready to get thin," George said.

Zorro turned to Joyce. "There is an observation booth in the OR. Would you care to watch?"

"Oh, yes," she said. "I watch surgeries all the time on the cable channels. The more blood the better as far as I'm concerned."

"Then you may be disappointed," Zorro said. "There is not much blood in this procedure. If you see a lot of it, something has gone wrong."

They wheeled George into the OR as a nurse guided Joyce to the observation booth. From above, she waved to him, and he was able to manage a short wave back before the anesthesia put him under. She watched them swab George with a dark liquid which, by virtue of the endless surgeries she had watched on TV, she knew to be a sterilizing solution. When they had connected him to the myriad of monitors with digital displays, Zorro hovered over the belly to make an incision.

A nurse handed him a round, thin object that was attached to a large machine nearby. The cannula. Zorro held it up and examined it in full light. He ran his gloved hand along the length. With the black cape flowing behind him, he did indeed look like a fencer with his foil; he looked to Joyce like . . . Zorro.

He eased the point of the cannula into the incision and began to probe. Joyce knew from their initial meeting with Zorro, Dr. Chin, that this cannula emitted ultrasound vibrations to break up the fat. For the first few minutes, Zorro stood stock still by the operating table, moving the wand up and down, in and out. Then his feet began to move, almost as if he was dancing in a shuffle step. She wondered if perhaps his feet had fallen asleep and he was attempting to restore circulation. It was only when he extended his left arm behind him that she realized what he was doing. He was jousting, as if his right hand held a sword and George's body was the opponent. His footwork was impressive, she thought. As he lunged and parried, she worried that all the movement would cause him to run George through, but his right arm and hand appeared steady. No one on the surgical team seemed to take any notice, so Joyce assumed this to be his standard method.

After thirty minutes of thrusts, he withdrew the cannula and inserted a different one. This was the suction device, and all the fat broken up by the ultrasound was now being sucked into the giant canister labelled Hoover beside the operating table. George was losing about a pound a minute. His kind of diet, thought Joyce. After an hour and half, Zorro withdrew the suction cannula for the last time, and with a flourish of his cape left the OR.

Chapter 44

George, 100 pounds lighter,
Wakes Up

George came out from under his liposuction anesthesia a very hungry man, but all they would give him in recovery was some water with a little sweetener. Joyce was there, of course, sending text messages on her IDrone to Kirstin and Scott that all had gone well.

"How did I do?" he asked her from his prone position on the gurney.

"Wonderfully," she assured, giving his hand a squeeze. "That is such an interesting procedure to watch, and that Dr. Chin has really got some style when it comes to surgery." Then she paused.

"What? Is something wrong?"

"I don't think so. It's just that I never saw him do the tummy tuck he said would come at the end."

"We'll ask him about that. The important thing is I'm a new man. When can we leave?"

Joyce was about to admit she didn't know when Zorro walked into the room without his cape. "How is our patient?" he asked.

"Hungry," George said. "And lighter."

"I'm afraid your diet will be all liquids for a few days."

"Gin is a liquid," George pointed out.

"That is true," said Zorro with a smile. "Your belly and love handles have experienced a lot of trauma, but as I promised, you are over one hundred pounds thinner. One hundred and three, to be precise. A personal record for me. You are going to feel incredibly sore when the medication wears off, so we will give you something for pain."

"Joyce was just telling me she didn't see you perform the plastic surgery at the end."

Zorro nodded. "Quite true. At the end of the procedure, I decided there were too many risks. You had been through a lot, you had been under anesthesia for a long time, and for a man with your health history and in your condition, I felt it better to stop when I did. We will deal with the excess skin in a separate operation when you have had some time to recover. Perhaps two months from now."

Joyce's face registered confusion. "What happens to the skin while we wait?"

"We cannot let it just hang, of course," said Zorro. "We will bind it to his body to give it support."

Now George looked puzzled. "You stitch it to

my body?"

Zorro laughed. "Oh, no. I don't know of any sutures strong enough to hold up that much skin. There is too much of it and it is too heavy. Remember, until today that same skin has been holding up and in over one hundred pounds. That is a lot of weight. Women in childbirth hold up twenty, thirty even forty pounds, but nothing like this."

"So how do you support it?" George asked.

"Duct tape."

Joyce said, "Don't worry, George. Your tux will cover it and Shawn will never know."

Chapter 45

Scott is suspended from school

Scott came home early from school, suspended.

"What for?" demanded Joyce, mentally gearing up to give someone a piece of her mind before knowing the reason.

"I forgot to take my gun."

"Oh, Scott. Honey, you know better than that."

"I left it on the counter in the computer lab, which for some reason was locked."

"So you couldn't take target practice with the kids?"

"Yeah. I shot some hoops instead."

"Couldn't someone loan you a gun?"

"Not a chance. They are like way strict on registrations. They expel anyone caught packing someone else's heat. Oh well, I can use the three days off."

"I hope the college admissions office doesn't hold this against you. They can get mighty picky these days."

Scott's misfortune arose as a result of last year's successful effort by Ammo America to require all students to carry handguns while on school grounds. According to Ammo America, this was a proven way to cut down on school violence. The results at Centerfield High had been mixed. On the plus side, the new policy eliminated the need for metal detectors, since every single student set them off every single day. The savings to the school system was substantial.

On the down side, a janitor had been shot in the leg on the first day of school by a nervous sophomore who swore he did not mean to pull the trigger. Fortunately the janitor, also armed, realized it was an accident and did not return fire. A junior shot himself in the buttock intending, he said, to extract his phone from his back pocket, but he mixed up the pockets and dialed the gun instead. Two girls in Scott's class got into a fight over a boy, and each brandished her revolver in the cafeteria. They were dealt with harshly by the administration. When Centerfield High had been renovated several years before one blackboard had been preserved, both as a memento of a bygone era and to facilitate the discipline meted out to these two pistol toting coeds, who were required to write on it five hundred times "I will not raise my weapon in anger." When contacted regarding these unfortunate incidences,

Ammo America spokesman Tex Bundy had responded that all new protections entailed adjustment, and that it sounded to him like changes needed to be made in the gun training program, a mandatory half hour before the school year started.

In fact, Centerfield no longer permitted physical education during school hours. The period formerly set aside for it was now used for target practice, the cost of which ate up all the savings from getting rid of metal detectors. Utilizing funds that had previously underwritten boys and girls soccer, a marksmanship team had been organized to compete with other schools, prompting a debate over whether cheerleaders would destroy the concentration of team members focused on the bullseye. A coach had been hired, an ex-con with a proven record of accuracy with handguns. But even the spirit of friendly competition with a rival school had proven problematic in an adjoining county, where the Travis High Terminators fought a close match with the Davis High Destroyers. The match came down to the final two shooters on the last target. With fans of both teams screaming and yelling, the Travis coach signaled for a time out just as the Davis shooter was about to fire his final, decisive round. Interviewed at the morgue after the match, the Travis coach said he merely intended to ice the shooter, but the Davis fans took it as bad sportsmanship and opened fire. Ammo America wasted no time in condemning the Davis fans, saying in a statement that

> Ammo America takes the dimmest possible view of the casualties resulting from the Travis-Davis match. We cannot allow the tradition of sport to be marred by such senseless behavior. Had match officials been sufficiently armed with automatic weapons, this type of violence could have been avoided. It is both logical and patently obvious that those in authority need firepower exceeding those over whom such authority is exercised. We remind all concerned that locking and loading are defensive measures designed to insure the safety of everyone, and that the decision to pull the trigger is one that can be made only after mature reflection of at least one second. Think before you shoot.

Joyce wondered if Scott's suspension might contain the seeds of a project worthy of SPHINCTER. What if, she asked herself, several handguns could be registered to the school library and checked out like books had been back in the day when students read books. Then any student forgetting or misplacing his or her weapon could be loaned a registered gun, thereby allowing such student to do his or her part to protect other students and to ensure school safety. She felt sure Ammo America would endorse the idea.

Chapter 46

Fran Hosts a dinner party

Fran's intent to host a dinner party was delayed so long by the still-yawning pit that she decided to go ahead with it. Lacking unlimited space in her modest rental house, she pared the guest list to those she most wished to see interact in a social setting. When George and Joyce received their invitation, they volunteered their home but Fran demurred, insisting she could accommodate the crowd, many of whom she expected to regret, though no one did.

From the paper she invited Ed and Wing, Kirstin and Jeff. She invited Buster and his wife despite the prospects, increasing daily, that she would challenge him in the next mayoral election. Art and Tricksy accepted "with pleasure" and Monty accepted on condition that Art not attend until a gelid frown from Fran made him change his mind. When Monty insisted that he not be the "token Arab," Fran invited the Abdullahs and then, to avoid offending the sole residents of New I, the Levys as well. She made it clear to Roger McCall that he was welcome to bring Olivia, but he said he would be coming alone. To Fran's profound surprise, Amos Albright accepted, indicating on his RSVP that he, too, would attend alone.

On the evening of the party, Chip parked cars to safeguard those not familiar with the risks posed by the pit. Fran greeted her guests at the door, steered them toward wine or soft drinks, and held her breath as she reminded herself that the Levys and the Abdullahs would be meeting for the first time.

Monty and the Abdullahs arrived first. In deference to their culture, she offered only soft drinks. Halim wore a plain, dark suit, while Hessa came dressed in a colorfully embroidered thawb, with a dark hijab pulled tightly around her head.

Next to arrive were Ed and Wing, arm in arm and mooning over each other like teenagers. George and Joyce, walking through the mesquite, came next, followed by Art, Tricksy, Chaim and Sonya Levy, who all came in the same car. Chaim wore a snappy open shirt and tailored blazer while his wife wore an off-the-shoulder silk cocktail dress. Tricksy's cowgirl outfit reminded Fran of Dale Evans except for the plunging neckline, the protruding cleavage, and the spiked heels. Next came Amos Albright, looking as forlorn as she remembered, nodding as he entered and accompanying his nod with a gift bottle of wine.

When Kirstin and Jeff came through the door, it was evident to Fran that they were under stress, but she later learned that the cause was not their personal relationship, which Kirstin confided had never been better, but Pete, who was again shadowing Kirstin. Roger McCall brought flowers, handing them to Fran with an odd little bow and a mischievous smile. Last to arrive was Buster, who entered with his usual swoosh and handed out autographed baseballs to every guest. Halim asked if he had an extra for Najair. Buster's wife, Consuelo, wore a stylized rebozo of costly, finely woven wool.

Now that all her guests had arrived, Fran circulated to make introductions, which proved possible for everyone except the New I and New P contingents, who hugged the walls of separate rooms. The din of conversation steadily increased as wine glasses were refilled. The formality of the new gave way to the easy drone of the familiar. At the hors d'oeuvres, George stood hoisting some delicious meatballs until he learned they were actually tofu, at which point he moved on to the skewered chicken, served with Ed's Barbecue Butter on the side.

When Fran felt a tug at her elbow, she turned to find Art standing there with a very serious look on his face. "I know this is a party," he said, "but I just learned something I think you should know."

"Don't tell me more rockets have landed," she said.

"There have been no further violations of New I's sovereignty, but I know who fired the bullet into the Abdullahs' trailer. As I thought, it was not the Levys. Today I went to see Mac Travis, one of my ranchers, about my option on his land. This happens to be the land where the Levys built their home. He said he had been hunting down by the arroyo. He did not realize anyone lived nearby, and of course he saw no need to ask permission to hunt on his own property. He felt very sorry about it."

Fran smiled. "Well, that is certainly good news. Have you informed the Abdullahs?"

"You mean speak to them? Directly?"

"Yes."

"Can't you do that?"

"I could, but I won't. I've spoken to them this evening. They seem like very nice people, as do the Levys. Why don't you just introduce yourself and tell them what you have learned?"

Art was rubbing his chin, mulling this suggestion, when Tricksy joined the conversation. He turned to her. "Fran thinks I should open direct negotiations with those people."

Fran glared. "I did not say anything about negotiations or mention 'those people.' I suggested you speak directly with the Abdullahs."

Tricksy said, "She that woman with the scarf wrapped around her head?"

"That is she," Fran confirmed.

Tricksy said, "I don't know who is giving her fashion advice, but she needs a second opinion. I'm going to give her the name of my hair stylist."

Before Fran could respond, Tricksy turned to seek out Hessa Abdullah, her spiked heels clicking on the floor as she went. "I have a bad feeling about this," Fran muttered to herself.

Hessa's time in Detroit had exposed her to a measure of western culture, but nothing had really prepared her for Texas tacky as practiced by Tricksy, who walked up, extended her jeweled hand, and said it was "right nice to meet her."

As Hessa stared at Tricksy's bulging cleavage, seemingly mesmerized, Tricksy said, "Girlfriend, I don't want to be forward or nothin' but who does your hair? We got to work on that. I gotta stylist that will make you look like a million bucks in an hour, two tops. And if you fall asleep under the hair dryer, you don't need to worry about him copping a cheap feel, if you get my drift, because he's as gay as a clutch purse at the Academy Awards. And he knows hair. Here in Texas we like the full-blown look. I'm bettin' you got some pretty locks under that head scarf." A speechless Hessa was still blushing when Art caught up to Tricksy.

"It is a cultural thing," Art explained. He introduced himself to Hessa and to Halim, who had joined them. When Monty approached, Art signaled to the Levys to join them.

When introductions were complete, Art related his conversation with Mac Travis and conveyed Travis's apology for the incident. "I guess I should have told the ranchers that there were people living out there."

Chaim Levy spoke next. "I am glad the cloud of suspicion has been lifted from us, as we would never do such a thing."

Halim said, "And we must apologize for the bottle rockets. My son is young, and we have been gone from Gaza so long he doesn't understand the significance."

Fran, who had been watching the exchanges from another room, ready at any moment to intervene if tensions escalated, began to relax as she saw conversations develop. As she joined the group,

Halim was asking Chaim about a problem Rayya was having with her permanent teeth coming in. Chaim, in turn, asked his advice about a clicking noise under the hood of his SUV. Hessa had yet to say anything, both because she still seemed stunned and because Tricksy had kept up a steady barrage of fashion advice, now directed at undergarments that "will make your titties stand up and be noticed, like mine."

Fran paid particular attention to Amos Albright, who upon arrival had headed straight to a corner nursing a glass of merlot. She took him by the elbow, guiding him from group to couple. It soon became apparent to her what Amos already knew, which was that he didn't know a soul there, and but for a couple of meetings which Buster had attended, had never seen them either.

As the cocktail hour drew to a close, Roger McCall approached Fran. Nodding subtly toward Kirstin across the room, he said, "Is that the woman you were telling me about? The one I'm too late for? She is a beauty."

Fran winked at him. "About Olivia's age, wouldn't you say?"

He nodded. "To be honest, I'm having a lot of trouble with girls--women--that age. The twenty-somethings. It is almost like they speak another language, and it isn't a language I have much interest in learning."

"And the women your own age?"

He shook his head, looking at the floor. "Married, most of them, or divorced with kids, which is okay, but not my first choice." Then he raised his head and looked directly at her. "Call this a shot in the dark, and I hope I'm not stepping across some line in asking, but would you like to go to a movie sometime?"

Fran hesitated, breaking off eye contact, before replying, "Yes. I would. That would be very . . . nice."

"I like movies," he said. "It is the one trivia category I excel at."

"I love them," she said, "but I never seem to make time to go. I'm afraid I've fallen into the habit of popcorn on the couch with a DVD. I haven't seen any of the current ones."

"Good," Roger said. "I'll call you. *The Moralist* is playing next week and I've heard good things about it. Great cast."

"I'm dying to see it," Fran said. "I read the book and Isabella Flynn is my favorite actress."

"Then we'll go. And we won't talk about the pit once. I promise."

Fran excused herself to serve dinner, and

accepted Roger's offer to help. When Kirstin and Jeff joined them, the meal appeared as if by sorcery.

When they were seated, Fran proposed a toast to "friends and Centerfield." George in turn proposed a toast to her as hostess. Chaim asked if the pork ribs were kosher, and when Fran said they were not, he said he didn't mind, he was just curious, because he didn't keep kosher anyway and he helped himself to three. Tricksy thought this meant he didn't use that funny salt she saw in the grocery store. Amos took a bite of the sweet potato soufflé and Fran thought she detected the faintest hint of a smile. Buster announced that the homemade habanero relish was the best he had ever tasted, including that made by his sainted grandmother, Josephina Bustamonte Nava.

For obvious reasons, two topics of conversation were implicitly off limits: middle eastern politics and the upcoming mayoral race. Amos surprised everyone by asking Roger to discuss his research into pre-Clovis artifacts. From the questions Amos asked, it became obvious to everyone, especially Roger, that Amos was quite knowledgeable on matters related to geology and anthropology. Roger apologized to those present for the inconvenience posed by the pit and tried to assure everyone that the potential for discovery, if realized, would more than justify their impatience and disgruntlement.

Joyce seized the opportunity to inform the group of Shawn Pen's visit, dropping hints that could not be considered veiled that he would be spending the night at the Fafalone residence. She urged those present to recommend worthy humanitarian projects for SPHINCTER's consideration and promised that all such proposals would be duly evaluated by her Truly Caring Persons Committee. George said he expected to have fully recovered from his liposuction by Shawn's visit and planned to greet his famous guest in a size forty-two jacket, which George had not worn since his mid-twenties. Joyce stood, walked to the end of the table, and took a photo of the dinner party with her IDrone. The phone flashed, the picture appeared, and in the Fafalone residence the ice maker shut off.

Chapter 47

Scott takes up a new hobby

Kirstin, on one of her weekly visits to her parents' home, asked about Scott.

"We never see him," said Joyce. "Spends all his time in his room. Ever since he went to that twelve-step thing he has been like a stranger."

George took a swig of his beer. "Ten to one he's up there on the computer downloading photos from assisted living websites."

"George!" said Joyce. "Your own son. Don't poke fun at his disability."

"I'll go up and see him," said Kirstin. "I miss him."

"Oh, he would love that," said Joyce.

Kirstin mounted the steps and walked down the hall leading to Scott's room. His door was closed, so she knocked.

"Stay out or die," came the voice from inside.

She opened the door. Scott looked up from a table in the middle of his room. On it rested an assortment of odd machines she didn't recognize.

"Hey, bro," she said.

"What's up, Sis? How's life in the soon-to-be-extinct art of journalism?"

"Great. I plan to ride the wooly mammoth to its grave. Did you ever look into that grave robbing problem I asked you about?"

"Oh, that. Forgot to tell you. They're stealing burial clothes. The Goths are advertising them as certified death garments at prices you would not believe."

"How bizarre is that? I was sure I'd catch you on the computer."

He glanced over at his desk, where his computer, flat screens, and assorted appendages rested. "I just use it now to check email."

"Are you ill? Our favorite mouse jockey is taking a break?"

He gave her the same smile he used to give her when he had conned Joyce into overlooking one of his misdemeanor antics. "It's still all about the mouse, but not that one," he said, pointing to his desk. "This one." He reached into the box in front of him and pulled out a white mouse by the tail. The mouse ran in place, looking for traction.

She put her hand on her right hip. "Okay, I'll bite. What's with the mouse? And what is all this stuff?"

Scott lowered the mouse back into the box. "Some design flaws in the mouse we need to take care of. And as soon as we take care of it, we can start on us."

"I'm lost."

"Computers are so yesterday," he said. "This is where it's happening. Your bro has hooked up with the biohackers. Coolest thing going."

"I'm afraid to ask, but what is a biohacker?"

"It's a biopunk without the advanced degree. Think of me as God."

"Why am I getting evil vibes from the term biohacker? What are you hacking?"

"Animal genomes. Tomorrow, the human genome. It's pretty cool now that the equipment is dirt cheap. Look at this awesome thermocycler I bought on EBay for $75. And how about this centrifuge? Ninety-five bucks."

"And why do you need a thermocycler?"

"To copy some DNA."

"Scott . . ."

"Okay, here's the deal. With advances in sequencing genes and with all this equipment available for practically nothing, anybody can splice some genes together to make something new. Like God. See the mouse?"

She walked closer and looked down into the box, where the mouse stood very still in a corner. "Yes?"

"The long tail has got to go. There is no reason for it except that's the way mice have been reproducing for thousands of years."

"Maybe there is a reason for it."

"Maybe, but who cares? It's a mouse."

"The mouse cares."

"So let's say the mouse is about to be run down by a cat. The cat can't reach anything but this long tail, but it pounces on that. Goodbye, mouse. But with a short tail, the cat comes up empty and daddy mouse gets to come home from work for another day."

"I see. Using some mouse genes and this equipment, you can breed a mouse with a shorter tail?"

"Or no tail. I get why a woman needs a tail, but why does a mouse need one?"

Kirstin grinned "You really are sick." Then, the grin vanished. "Aren't you afraid of creating something really freaky? Maybe even dangerous?"

He shrugged. "Everything has a risk."

"Does this have any practical application?"

"As a matter of fact, it does, or it might. I think

my shoe fetish is genetic. Some gene got mutated along the way and I'm suffering because of it. When I learn enough about this genetics business, I'm going to solve my own problem. But one step at a time. First I have to bob this mouse's tail."

"And after that?"

"Seedless grapes."

"That's been done."

"Okay, seedless seeds. I'll think of something."

Chapter 48

Fran and Roger See More than the Movie

After her dinner party, Fran reflected on Roger's promise to call her for a movie and predicted he would not. When he did, she permitted herself the ego boost that came from being asked out by a younger man who was not only bright but so easy on the eyes. Once she agreed to pizza and a movie, she looked forward to it, surprised that something so casual could produce the slight nervousness she felt. She had her hair done and wore a cashmere sweater that accented her modest cleavage.

He arrived to pick her up in his best denim shirt and pressed jeans. For the hour before the show began, they shared a large pizza (her half Hawaiian and his with extra cheese) and each ordered a beer. He told her a joke one of his students had related that made her laugh ("Two archaeologists walk into a bar. Nothing happens for a thousand years.") She told him about the last movie she had seen in a theater, three years before, and warned him she cried in sad spots without embarrassment.

"You said you read *The Moralist*," he said. "Were there sad spots?"

"Just a couple, but it was the middle of my election campaign and perhaps I missed more. I don't think I've ever read a book where absolutely nothing sad happens, even when the book is funny like *The Moralist*."

"Or the screenwriter may have taken liberties with the script," he offered. "They love doing that."

"If Isabella Flynn is in it, I'm not worried. I'd pay to watch her sit on the set for an hour and a half."

"She's very special," he agreed. "Did you see her in *One October Night*? Fabulous performance. She carried the film."

They chatted on about her job and his education. When it was time to go, she regretted the movie started so soon. At her insistence they split the check, but she let him buy her ticket. She bought popcorn they shared. Holding it occupied her hands, which she was glad about since she found herself wondering if he would try to hold her hand, and whether, if he did, she would let him. But the movie ended with no more physical contact between them than the accidental touching of elbows when they were both laughing. At one point she leaned close to whisper that she wasn't sure she had ever seen Isabella Flynn in a comedic role before. The aroma of his aftershave gave her a pleasing little jolt.

Back at Fran's, he walked her to her door. She started to ask him in, then thought better of it. He took her hand in what could have been a handshake but could have been more, staring at her with his blue eyes. She wanted him to kiss her, but he hesitated, then said goodnight in a way that left her feeling as if he had kissed her. Almost.

Chapter 49

Fran's Big Day
(and Bigger Night)

Fran waited for Buster to announce his reelection bid before declaring herself officially in the race. To an overflow crowd assembled on the steps of City Hall, she pledged to lead Centerfield "to the next progressive level," emphasizing themes that her editorials had underscored her passion for; education, child welfare, public safety, and the park. She criticized neither Buster nor his policies, preferring to strike a positive chord. His reelection slogan, "More good things, si, Bad things no," presented a fat target for ridicule, summoning all the restraint she and her advisors could muster. She assured voters that she would relinquish her editorial duties, but not her managerial duties, for her time in office.

When she had concluded her speech, she stepped down into the crowd to greet personally each of those who had come to hear her. Among the last was Roger McCall, who shook her hand with a wry smile and told her she looked like she could use a beer.

"If that's an invitation," she said, "you're on."

In the weeks leading up to her announcement, she and Roger had been to the movies several times. Yet for reasons never articulated by either, they had avoided going out to eat, taking drives into the country, or doing anything more intimate than sitting together in a dark theater appraising the film or critiquing the actors. Somehow, the movie habit wasn't dating, and dating was evidently not comfortable. Perhaps it was their age difference, or Roger's daily presence at the pit, where Olivia still batted her eyes and other assets at him. Whatever the rationale, it was about to be tested, because Roger asked her to dinner.

They went to a small Italian restaurant, the Reeva Derchi, that had recently opened and that *The Sentinel* had favorably reviewed. Over a chianti selected by Roger, they toasted Fran's performance and the impressive crowd that came to watch it.

"I think you're going to win," Roger predicted.

"I'll bet you say that to all the girls."

"To all the women I know running for mayor? You happen to be in a league of your own there."

"Let's not count chickens," she said. "Buster has lots of friends out there." She paused, and then with a lowered voice said, "Some of them aren't even named Bustamonte." When Roger laughed she said, "If you quote me I'll deny it."

"You're safe with me," he said casually.

She looked at him directly, and far less casually. "You know, I believe you."

"Yeah? On what basis?"

"On the basis of watching eight or ten films with you and listening to the things you like and don't like. You seem to focus on values, and that is a sign of trust, at least to me."

He nodded thoughtfully. "I'll remember that."

They talked about films, the dig in the pit, Chip's ability to wash so many cars in such a short time (Fran: "If he keeps this up he won't be able to afford to go off to college because he's getting rich washing cars"), Olivia's persistent crush. Before either knew it, the meal was over and dessert in front of them.

Fran shocked herself by saying, "I've never seen your apartment."

Roger looked momentarily stunned. He put his napkin to his lips and took a sip of wine.

"Is that too forward?" she asked.

"Not at all. I've been working up the courage to ask you. So, would you like to see my apartment?"

"I would."

They drove to his place holding hands over the console. At the front door, he stepped aside to let her in. When he closed the door and turned around, she was standing there looking up at him longingly. Their first kiss was long, deep and intense, as was the lovemaking that followed. Fran left two hours later, deliciously exhausted and giggling at that reality that announcing for mayor was only the second most exciting thing she had done that day.

Chapter 50

Shawn Pen comes to town

It seemed to Joyce that the day for Shawn Pen's visit would never arrive. For the week preceding it, she paced her living room floor, trying to anticipate his every need for the twenty-four hours of his scheduled stay. Every time a text message hit her IDrone, she felt certain it was to inform her that some humanitarian crisis had arisen in Kuala Lumpur or Mogadishu that made Shawn's presence there essential. But the day before he was to arrive, she received a final confirmatory email from his advance team fine-tuning his itinerary. This was actually going to happen, she told herself and everyone else who would listen. Best of all, her determination that he would spend the night at the Fafalone residence had paid off. He had accepted her "kind invitation with pleasure."

His advance team shrewdly made his first stop at *The Sentinel*, for an interview Fran looked forward to. She had braced herself against being drawn into his orbit, magnetized by star power she privately discounted. He was just a man, she reminded herself, and probably a short one. They all seemed short in the flesh.

She met him in the reception area. His handshake was firm, his eyes blue and piercing, and against her will her knees trembled as she led him into her office, where Kirstin awaited to take notes.

"Mr. Pen," Fran said, "welcome to Centerfield."

"Call me Shawn," he said, "and the pleasure is all mine."

Fran glanced at Kirstin, who did her best to appear restrained and professional. For the first time it occurred to Kirstin that her mother may have been right on this one.

"I'll be seeing you this evening at the reception," Fran said. "I look forward to telling you what a big fan I am of your work and perhaps even asking you about your role in a favorite film or two, but that can wait for the social hour. At the moment I'm interested in the humanitarian work being carried out by your foundation, which I believe is called SPHINCTER."

"We're on every continent now," he said with an air of deference. "We look for the special problems no one else seems to be addressing."

"Can you give me an example of one you are particularly excited about?"

"Sure. You may have read that bread consumption in France has reached a dangerously low level. I personally witnessed this at Cannes last year. I remember telling Steven Spielberg that it had all the earmarks of an impending crisis. I've been doing this work long enough now to smell a crisis in its infancy. As soon as I accepted my award, I returned to the U.S. to mobilize the resources of SPHINCTER."

"And what action, precisely, did you take?"

"We began a public awareness campaign, highlighting the role of bread in French history, beginning with that loaf stolen by Jean Valjean. We reminded the people of Marie Antoinette's famous quote to 'let them eat bread.'"

"I thought that was cake, and that it was the lack of bread that spawned the Revolution." Fran said.

"I've heard that theory expressed, but it worked better for our purposes that the quote feature bread. And cake has all that gluten we want to discourage."

"I see. And the medium for getting your message out?"

"The younger French are very social media savvy, so we bombarded them with Tweets and Facebook postings. That was the easy part. But statistics show that the greatest decline in bread consumption has been in the rural areas, where the population is much older and is definitely not plugged into the world wide web."

"And how did you reach them?"

"We borrowed a page out of World War II and dropped leaflets all over the country. Twenty million fliers, all in French of course."

Fran feared her skepticism was obvious. "Did anyone raise the issue of littering?"

"Oh, the usual bureaucrats, but they were the same ones who left Paris in the hands of the Nazis. We considered dropping actual loaves of bread. Whole gain, of course. I mean, what could send a better message than giving them the product literally on their doorsteps?"

"But you opted for the fliers . . ."

"Because I was reminded of how lousy the weather is in France, and if it rained, as it usually does, the bread would get soggy."

"And how would all those fliers do when it rained? I'm not being argumentative, just curious."

"Good question, but SPHINCTER doesn't like to be behind the times. We try to stay ahead, which is why I insisted on biodegradable paper. In ten years there won't be a shred of it left."

Fran nodded, thinking it best to move on. "And to what does Centerfield owe the honor of this visit?"

"You have one of the most active chapters of SPHINCTER in our organization. A woman named Joyce Fafalone. Do you know her?"

"Joyce and George are my next-door neighbors. And they also happen to be Kirstin's parents." Fran and Kirstin exchanged smiles.

Shawn looked at Kirstin. "Your mother is someone I want to meet," he said. "She has been very generous in her support and so active in recruiting new members."

Kirstin winked at Fran while telling Shawn, "I think she's a bit star struck."

"All for a good cause. I should say causes because on the jet coming in I reviewed the worthy projects her chapter has proposed. That 'Adopt an Indian Landfill' initiative has real possibilities."

"I believe that's her personal favorite, too. Maybe because it was her idea," Kirstin said. "I think the plan to deliver mail there may have to be tweaked."

"That's what I love about this work," Shawn replied. "The challenges to relieving human suffering are endless, but the rewards are also endless."

Fran asked, "And what would you say is your

biggest challenge in this work?"

"Governments. It's always the politicians with their hands out."

Fran stood. "Well, Shawn, I'm running for mayor here, and if I'm elected my hand will be out for the sole purpose of welcoming you back to Centerfield any time you wish to come."

Chapter 51

The Fafalones entertain
Shawn Pen

George and Joyce argued about the red carpet for weeks before Shawn Pen's visit. George insisted that red carpets were reserved for those chest-thumping awards shows Hollywood loved to throw, where each star could outshine the other while secretly wishing their rivals would trip falling out of the limo. Joyce firmly stated and repeated that she viewed hosting Shawn as a once-in-a-lifetime experience and that a red carpet was essential to set the proper tone for his visit. George eventually gave in, telling her to order what she needed.

That turned out to be quite a bit; just under a quarter of a mile of red carpet. On the day their celebrity guest arrived, the catering company rolled out the carpet from the front door, down the steps, across the driveway, through the security gate, and into the mesquite trees, where it meandered in a serpentine path that eventually skirted the pit and ended at the special parking spot where the limo, on loan from George's funeral home, was expected to deposit the special guest.

The red-carpet dispute paled beside the argument over Shawn's bottled water. His advance team specified that his room be stocked with two bottles of Aquagold, which turned out to spring from a single source--a well in rural Belgium. Joyce wanted to order a case ("Suppose he decides to stay a week?") while George insisted that two bottles were sufficient, particularly when a case cost $385 and with priority shipping from Brussels came to a tidy $550. George railed about the wolf at the door, but if the wolf really was at the door, it must have been at the front door because Joyce went through the back door and ordered it anyway.

Then there were the issues related to the reception guest list. Citing expense, George wanted it limited to fifty, but his business contacts alone took up half of that quota and Joyce said she would compromise at two hundred. She invited all her committee members, her bridge club, her book club, her church axillary, the city council, and selected neighbors including Fran. Joyce told Fran to invite "anyone you want," so she invited Art and Tricksy, Monty, the Levys, the Abdullahs, Amos Albright, and of course Roger McCall. Every person invited accepted.

At 5:30 p.m. on the big day, Joyce and George made their way to parking lot in anticipation of Shawn's arrival at 6. George wore a dark double-breasted blazer that served to both exhibit his new slenderness but also to conceal the duct tape that held his skin in place. Joyce wore a chic dress with a floral design she had spent a day shopping in Houston for. Standing at the parking space, Joyce lamented not having something to calm her nerves and George suggested the double vodka had worked well for him.

At precisely 6, the limo pulled up and Shawn emerged. Joyce felt faint but stayed upright, determined to restrain herself for at least thirty seconds before telling him how THRILLED they were to welcome him. As an aide removed luggage from the trunk of the limo, George and Joyce led Shawn on the serpentine path toward the house. If Shawn found the red carpet unusual, he didn't say so. George explained the pit and the obstacles to filling it in while Joyce gazed at Shawn.

Once inside the Fafalone residence, they showed Shawn to his room. He closed the door to take a power nap, drink some Aquagold, and dress for the party.

Guests began arriving at seven. By eight,

everyone invited was present, many on their second and even third drink. Buster sat in a corner signing baseballs as everyone else kept an eye on the stairs for Shawn's appearance. At 8:15 he descended, dressed in black chinos, a black silk shirt, and a black jacket. George wisecracked under his breath about Shawn's color coordination as Joyce rushed to him. He accepted a proffered glass of white wine and accompanied Joyce as she introduced him to her guests. When they came to Fran, Shawn smiled in acknowledgement and said he was ready to talk with her about his films if she was still interested. A crowd pressed around them as he signed autographs and posed for photos. He even signed a baseball for Buster.

Art and Tricksy had arrived with Chaim and Sonia Levy and greeted Monty and the Abdullahs, who were already inside. The fact that they had all meet and spoken at Fran's party significantly diffused what might otherwise have proved awkward. While awaiting Shawn's appearance, the New I contingent stayed in the dining room while Monty and the Abdullahs lingered in the living room. But Shawn's magnetism drew friend and foe, and eventually they found themselves together, chatting about movies.

At ten, Tricksy announced she had to be at work at The North Pole in half an hour. The party was winding down, so people started leaving, clutching their autographs and emailing photos of themselves with Shawn. Fran and Roger started to leave when Art suggested they accompany him to the North Pole. Fran turned to Roger and shrugged. He shrugged back.

Fran said, "Maybe Ed and Wing would like to join us. I'll ask them."

When she returned to announce that Ed and Wing were game, Art shocked everyone by suggesting that Monty and the Abdullahs might also like to go.

Monty said, "That is a very thoughtful gesture, Art, and speaking only for myself I accept. But you must remember I am a man of the world, and I have lived in the U.S. for many years. The Abdullahs, on the other hand, are not nearly so worldly. With all due respect to Tricksy's talent and line of work, I do not think the Abdullahs would be entertained by what goes on at The North Pole."

Art nodded before saying, "Why don't you ask them?"

Monty replied, "I guess it can't hurt. They will feel included for having been invited." He left, returning minutes later, wide-eyed. "They want to go."

Tricksy said, "The more the merrier, but I hoped you warned Mrs. Abdullah. She has on more clothes tonight than I wear at The North Pole in a month."

Monty said to Tricksy, "You may not have noticed me in the crowds because you were . . . busy, but I have seen your show twice. I have warned Hessa, Mrs. Abdullah, what to expect. She insists that she is not as sheltered as you might think. Remember, she came here from Detroit."

After saying their goodbyes to George, Joyce and Shawn, the unlikely companions headed to The North Pole, where Tricksy excused herself to dress.

"Well," she said to Sonia, "when I say I'm getting dressed, I'm getting undressed, but you know what I mean."

Near the runway, Art arranged for a table large enough to accommodate Ed and Wing, Fran and Roger, Chaim and Sonia, Halim and Hessa, Monty and himself.

"The first round is on me," Art announced.

Everyone ordered a drink except for Halim and Hessa. "We do not believe in drinking spirits," said Halim.

"You've never had a drink?" asked Ed. "That's downright un-American, and you're in America. If you're not going to drink, why did we bother to repeal the Fifth Amendment about prohibition?"

"Ed," Fran said gently, "the Fifth Amendment is alive and well, and it protects your right to remain silent."

"Why would I do that? I'm sayin' it's a Texan's birthright to drink what he wants when he wants, and even though Halim here is an A-rab, he's become an honorary Texan by moving to Centerfield, opening a business, and selling guns to people who can pay for them."

Monty turned to Halim. "We won't pressure you, my friend, but let me assure you that what our people say in public and what they do in private are two very different things. Liquor flows like oil in places that would shock you."

Halim rubbed his chin. "I must admit I have been curious about it."

"Then order one," said Ed. "Be a Texan. Order two."

Halim looked at Hessa, who grinned and said, "It is up to you. I can drive if you are worried about that."

Halim raised his hands as if surrendering.

"Well, I guess there's no time like now. What should I order?"

"Maybe bourbon and ginger," suggested Monty.

Ed scoffed. "Bourbon and ginger? He might as well order a Shirley Temple. When a man takes his first drink, he needs a real drink. Leave this to me." Ed motioned to a waiter, who returned minutes later to set in front of Halim a short glass of clear liquid.

"What is it?" asked Halim.

"Mescal," said Ed. "Comes from cactus."

Everyone watched as Halim took a tepid sip. He winced.

"Good, eh?" said Ed.

"Very strong," said Halim. His eyes watered. He turned to offer Hessa a sip. She shook her head decisively.

Applause erupted as Tricksy made her entrance, gliding down the pole with one arm spread in ballerina precision and grace. Art stood and whistled. To everyone's surprise, Hessa clapped.

Halim took another sip of his mescal. He wasn't sure how much of the show he should watch, but Hessa seemed engaged in Tricksy's gyrations, which he took as a license to ogle. So he took another sip and studied her moves as she thrust her hips and embraced the pole with phallic intensity. By the time Ed ordered the next round, Halim had drained his mescal and signaled for another.

Art turned to Chaim and Sonia, both of whom nursed draft beers as they watched the show. Sonia clucked, "How old did you say Tricksy is? That is quite a body for a woman her age. Any age, really."

Ed said, "Chaim, Halim just ordered his second mescal. Are you in?"

"I'm not much of a drinker. Bad for the teeth."

Ed looked indignant. "Where's your pride, man? Halim here never had a drink in his life until twenty minutes ago. You gonna let an A-rab outdo you on a matter as important as this?"

Chaim cast a sideways glance at Sonia before saying, "I guess one mescal won't hurt the teeth. I can brush when I get home."

"That's the spirit," Ed said.

Over the music, Fran asked no one in particular what they thought of Shawn Pen.

"So handsome," said Sonia.

"I have never seen one of his movies," Hessa said, "but now I will see them all."

"I marry him," said Wing.

"Not so fast," Ed told her. "You promised me."

When the waiter set down the second round of

drinks, Ed raised his glass. "To Centerfield, to Texas," he toasted, then drained his glass with a satisfied "ahhh." Everyone raised a glass and nodded his way.

Art said, "Excuse me while I go to the runway and show my appreciation. The nice thing about giving Tricksy five-dollar bills is that they all end up at our house at the end of the night."

"Wait," said Halim. "I will go with you. Another new experience." Hessa rolled her eyes but remained silent.

"I'll go, too," said Chaim. "A performance as artistic as that one deserves reward."

Sonia said, "I thought you always said you can't put a price on art."

Chaim looked momentarily sheepish. "Some art lends itself to ones and fives."

At the runway, Art placed his arm around Halim's shoulders and said, "Watch and learn," as Chaim looked on.

Tricksy, seeing them pressing forward in the crowd, strolled her bump and grind their way. When she reached Art, she dropped to her knees, swinging her left breast clockwise, the right one counterclockwise as the tassels flew. Chaim and Halim exchanged looks. "That is truly remarkable,"

Chaim allowed, and Halim nodded his agreement.

"Worthy of a five spot," Art said, tucking the bill into the fringe of her g-string.

Halim, eyes wide, followed his lead. Not to be outdone, Chaim placed a five at each hip. Tricksy leaned down to plant a kiss on the forehead of each donor before continuing her stroll as anxious cowboys waved money at her like bidders at an auction, which in a sense, they were. Chaim ran out of fives and asked Halim for change.

Back at the tables, Fran observed that boys will be boys, a statement that met with general agreement from the women. She urged Roger to join the men if he wished, but he just smiled and sipped his beer.

The show ended with Tricksy's signature number. To the tune of God Bless America, she hung upside down on the pole, her legs spread-eagled and her free arm saluting the U.S. and her patrons at the runway.

When the men returned to the tables, Monty said he had the next round covered.

"Oh, no," said Art, "I've got this one."

"Absolutely not," said Monty. "This one's on me."

Fran raised her hand. "Gentlemen, this

reminds me of the argument over which conference room would host the first meeting. Surely there is a way to work this out."

To general laughter, Monty said, "Of course I will defer to my friend, Art, provided he agrees that the round following his will be mine."

Art said, "A generous gesture freely accepted."

Halim, beginning to show the effects of the mescal, asked Chaim if it would suit him and Sonia for the Abdullahs to visit, as they wished to see the house he had heard so much about. "And I apologize once again for the rockets."

"You are welcome anytime," Sonia said.

"And we feel badly for overreacting," Chaim added, slurring "badly" into something closer to "baddy" as the mescal took its toll.

Ed, seeing a slim window for world peace open, asked everyone for a toast.

Chaim stood first, however unsteadily. "To New Palestine," he said. "May we live in peace as neighbors."

Halim followed, raising his mescal and spilling half of it. "To New Israel. May our bonds as Texans hold us together come what may."

Ed stood next. "To Fran, our new mayor. May our fair city be known henceforth for something other than baseball."

Fran took her turn next. "To Amos Albright, whose gift of land for the park has launched my administration on such a positive note."

Art rose to his feet. "To the fabulous Tricksy," he said. "And to the day Texas secedes from the Union."

Everyone cheered except Fran, who could only shake her head and grip Roger's hand tighter under the table.

So we must leave Centerfield. If you go there today, you will find a world class public park, welcomed by a giant statue of Amos Albright, dressed as a clown and making others happy as he did for the length of his career. *The Sentinel* is a daily on-line paper, with Fran as its editor, now in her second term as mayor. She and Roger recently became engaged but haven't set the date yet. Kirstin and Jeff married and are expecting a child. Scott got serious about his grades, went to Stanford, and has recently been hired by Google. Joyce continues her work with SPHINCTER and is said to text Shawn Pen on a daily basis, despite the fact that the Fafalone oven occasionally sets itself to 375 degrees when she hits the "send" button. George sold the cemetery, kept the funeral home, and has also managed to keep off most of the weight. The pit still yawns at the end of Fran's driveway.

Texas remains in the Union, but there are rumors . . .

# # #